Dedication

*For the Mountains I grew up in the north.
A huge thank you to my loving &
supportive husband, Alexander.L.Gresl,
who is always encouraging me to follow
my heart & dreams. I love you.
To my grandparents, Vital and Eliza Clille.
Whose teachings are the inspiration behind
my stories.
Thank you for always being there &
believing in me.*

Shúhta Dene: Go'diah's Quest
Maureen Gresl

Print ISBNs
Amazon print 9780228635437
Ingram Spark 9780228633839
Barnes & Noble 9780228635413
BWL Print 9780228633846

Paranormal Canadiana Collection
Copyright 2025 BWL Publishing Inc.
Copyright 2025 by Maureen Gresl
Editor Nancy M Bell
Cover artist Michelle Lee

The Paranormal Canadiana Collection

Night at the Legislature – Manitoba – Author Nancy M. Bell

Shúhta Dene – Northwest Territories – author Maureen Gresl

Astrophobia – Saskatchewan – author Paul Grant

Dancing Mary – British Columbia – author Jay Lang Young

Twice born – New Brunswick – author Graeme Smith

Playtime – Prince Edward Island – author Eden Monroe

Black Gold Eye - Alberta – author JD Shipton

2026 Releases

Ghosts of Bell Island - Newfoundland - Eileen Charbonneau and Jude Pittman

Haunting the Klondike - Yukon – author Joan Donaldson-Yarmey

Cardinal - Nova Scotia – author donalee Moulton

The Deepest Divide - Ontario – JC Kavanagh

Metamorphe - Quebec – author Juliet Waldron
with John Wisdomkeeper (posthumously)

Table of Contents

Part One

Shúhta Dene
The Mountain

Chapter One

Stories and legends tell of a medicine woman, banished from her village as a witch. The tales of wonderous gifts of healing medicine make a young woman determined to find those legendary healing plants and the medicine woman, if the stories are true. She is desperate to find her dying grandfather a cure before he goes mad from dreams. With the blessing of her elders, she sets off with her dog, Midnight, to find what she seeks.

The young woman must first find her own way through the mountains, and journey through visions and nightmares to find her own answers. She must conquer the old trails rich with tales of things that make you lose yourself, or your mind. Finally, she is required to face what she never expected to find......

* * *

I'm Go'diah. I was raised by my grandparents on the land in a small remote village nestled between the mountains and the river that travels through the whole of the north. They taught me the ways of our culture, how to live and survive, what plants and berries to avoid, what animals to eat, and which to stay away from. Everything was always about respecting nature, balance, meditations, taking only what is needed.

The mountains run far back, a wide stretch of lands, untouched and remote, with trails that reach into the dark, forest covered mountains. These trails were marked by the elders long before, forking in many directions. Dangerous to those unfamiliar with the markings.

The children were taught by the elders to carry the tradition to the next generation, but the stories passed down by the few who lived to tell of their exploration of the mountains lead me to my story.

The story begins

Beda, my grandpa, had just left for his seasonal hunt. I was seventeen and worried about him as he wasn't feeling well. In spite of that, I knew he would go, as it was his job. Fall was well advanced, and the winter was coming in a little faster than usual this year.

Moonlight, my grandma, was busy making jam, drying herbs, and preparing dried meat for the winter. In her spare time, between cooking and caring for us she was making slippers for my grandpa as a surprise for Christmas with matching fur gloves.

Uncle John stayed at home from the hunting to help. It was up to him to oversee the winter preparations, making sure we had enough wood for the winter, gathering, cutting, and stockpiling it in the woodshed. He was often gone for days on end.

I went to school and helped my grandma, Moonlight, with the chores. When I was needed, I worked at the community store for extra money to help our household. This was my last year of schooling here before I left to pursue further education elsewhere. I was excited for the upcoming school dance and a chance to take some time to myself before preparing to leave. My best friend, and a few cousins of course, you know the group, hung out by the fire, telling scary stories, roasting marshmallows and staying out past curfew. Well, my little group told stories and played dare.

The dance was over at 10pm as no one is allowed out past midnight in the community. There were spooky tales of shadow people that creeped around in the night to prey on our dogs and had been known to take children. Just stories, but it was never wise to disrespect the elders' stories. We left the hall and headed to the riverbanks to make our fire and tell our stories. Every time we get together in a group we try to outdo each other with who can tell the scariest stories, before midnight. This year it was different. We told our stories, but we all agreed that there was one story all our stories were based on. Witch Mountain. Legends and stories told of a woman who was banished from her village after being accused of being a witch. She never aged they said, and young ones went missing every few years. Just legends and stories, we told ourselves.

After that night, I started thinking about the trails all over the mountains. If the stories were even a bit true, this witch woman might even know some healing plants that could help some of our sick elders, like my grandpa. Beda is a hunter and trapper. He got sick this past summer and is slowly dying. He has been travelling all over the lands, hunting and looking for medicines of the land to cure his condition. The sickness worsens as winter heads in. Beda claims to see a woman in his dreams and fears he might go mad with dreams and searching.

I will be eighteen in a few months. I plan to undertake a journey of my own by the spring, surviving on the land, it will be my initiation into adulthood. I will go with the blessings of the elders, so I have started planning. I spend time with all the elders, gathering stories and creating a map based on those stories. Many of the elders are sick, like my grandpa, and the sickness makes me wonder if there is some underlying reason we don't know about.

There is much to do and prepare. Christmas has come and gone. I celebrated my birthday and became a woman in my own right. The elders bestowed their blessings, and they gave me a gift. Sage for protection on my journey to seek out medicine and answers for my elders. I was so excited. I had packed and planned for months ready to wake and begin my journey. I worried about my grandpa and prayed he would last a few more years, he was our provider.

When I was only six years old he took my hand and we walked the trail. He spoke of the land, how it provided for everything we would ever need, and how we are responsible for showing respect to the gifts it gives us. The earth, water, wind and sky, the animals, fish and plants. Everything is part of a balance, a circle, and we are part of it.

We spent so many days and nights, as he taught me, what it meant to be a part of mother earth. Each night, he told stories of the elders, those who have passed on, but still watch over us and how some nights they will come to you. They dance high in the heavens, and as they dance their moccasin's make the northern lights. If you listen, once in a while, you can hear them sing.

His visions have led to powerful dreams--visions, that as I grew older, became so clear. Visions of places I have never been, faces I have never seen, bring me comfort and my grandpa said they were helping me, showing me my path for the future.

Since my grandpa started getting sick, the visions have been beyond powerful and so real, I have woken screaming. These visions have led my path, have started my journey. This feeling of where to go is now too strong to ignore, and important that I follow for my grandpa and my people.

That first spring morning, I was so excited, the birds were out singing, the ice on the house melting. I could hear music of water falling into the puddles under my window. The early flies were sitting in the sun on the side of the house, the air so warm and bright with the scent of spring in the breeze filling my lungs with cool fresh air. It made me love just being alive. The smell of Grandpa's fresh brewed coffee, and bacon cooking was glorious. I stretched and washed up, got my stuff and pack ready by the door. Grandpa looked worried, he had a gun with a bag of shells waiting for me with already packed meals and water for the trip. We sat and drank coffee on the porch savoring a moment of silence to take it all in. Grandpa gave me a lot of tips on what to look for and how to mark my way, he said I was a woman now and the journey was mine to make.

He cried as I hugged him and Grandma goodbye. Uncle shoved smokes and a bag of orange ribbons in my backpack while telling me how proud they all were of me. Grandpa and Uncle would come search for me in 12 days' time if I have put the markers up correctly, they would find me.

As I said goodbye, they all came out to see me. I whistled for my dog Midnight to come with me. I took the heaviest steps of my entire life as I crested the rise at the top of the trail, turned to where they were all still waving and walked over the hill without looking back.

I walked for a good while before my back started hurting from the heavy pack. Midnight was keeping up and marking his territory. I followed my grandpa's trail to the fork he had described to me.

I listened as I walked, and watched where I stepped, in case I bumped into any unwanted guests, like bears. Midnight was with me, big and black just like a bear in the shadows. He stayed by my side and jumped at every squirrel in the trees, he was a good hunting dog. My uncle trained him for me, mainly that dog loved the rabbits. Grandpa gave Midnight to me as a birthday gift one year and the puppy grew with me. Grandma named him Midnight, because as a puppy, he used to blend into the dark.

The sun was going down making it muggy in the depth of the thick forest. I hadn't been up here since I was a child, my grandparents used to take me hunting for rabbits and we'd camp out at the fork. Grandpa would tell stories before bed, beautiful memories I cherished. I found the camp site by 5:30, so I started setting up my camp for the night. I set up my tent and laid out my sleeping bag. I remembered Grandpa telling me to start my fire first thing and keep it going through the night. I started gathering up wood, there was an old wood pile nearby, but it was so dried and old I realized that hardly anyone used these trails. Which was surprising as it was just about a day's walk to get there.

Midnight jumped in the tent as the night-time coldness set in. Snow still lay on the ground through the trees, glimmering ghostlike in the gathering dusk. I piled fuel on the fire making it nice and big. I settled down and pulled out the sandwiches, apple, and dried meat Grandma had packed. She'd provided all dried foods and herbs for my journey, so I wouldn't need to cook too much, for me or the dog. She was always thinking of us. The temperature dropped fast under the trees. I laid the gun by my side, threw a few more logs on the fire, before crawling into my tent, taking the gun with me. I set me and Midnight up for the night. I had my flashlight, my book, and shared some food with my dog. I bundled up in the parka I packed in anticipation of the cold nights and I fell asleep with Midnight curled beside me.

My face was cold and somewhere an alarm was sounding. Was it morning already? I could swear I just closed my eyes.

Crawling to the tent door, I unzipped it and looked outside. It was pitch dark still. How could that be? Everything moved in slow motion, what was going on? Was I dreaming? It seemed too real to be a dream. I listened but couldn't hear a thing. My ears were ringing, a loud pitch high sound drilling into my skull. I closed my eyes and silence descended. I could hear the watch, the tic-tock of the hand. Somehow it grew louder and slower. I shook my head and looked at Midnight. Except it wasn't Midnight, but a Big Black Wolf who lunged and attacked my face. I screamed so hard I woke up myself up. I lay back on my sleeping bag, breathing rapidly. What a flipping dream. My heart pounded and sweat soaked my hair. Midnight was still out cold, sleeping on his back, undisturbed by my scream. Maybe I didn't scream except in my dream? I took a deep breath and gulped some water. I checked my watch. Three in the morning. OMG, only three more hours of sleep before I had move on. I have to keep on track. I laid back down wondering if maybe that dream manifested because I was thinking of Midnight and I'm a little scared of wolves. I closed my eyes and let myself drift into a deep sleep.

Chapter Two

Day 2 ~Alarm goes off~8:am

The dog was whining to go out, so I unzipped the tent door and let him out. I stretched, my body complaining about the unfamiliar bed. Oh my God, my back hurt from a root I slept on. I crawled out of the tent, barely moving, and threw more wood on the fire. Thank goodness the coals were still glowing. I waited until the new wood caught then put my coffee pot deep in the coals. I couldn't wait for that first cup of coffee outside on a spring morning. Midnight jumped back in the tent and watched from the blanket. I poured my cup, mixed it and had my first sip with a smoke. Leaning back, I started planning my day, mapping out which way I wanted to go. While I was deciding I cooked some eggs to go with my Bannock. What great ingredients for a meal. I packed up as the sun grew stronger, slanting down through the trees. I got my pack ready, map in hand and a handful of ribbons ready to mark my path. I was full of breakfast and boundless energy.

The fork on the trail

I checked the map. Three trails branched off from the fork. The one on the left was a little grown in and looked like it might lead down the mountain, the trail straight ahead of me seemed to have had more use and headed upward, the one on the right side appeared more grown in but looked like it might be going up the right side of the mountain and maybe over it? Something in me said go right. The choice was mine to make now. As my grandfather would say, now my journey begins, and I must choose wisely, or I too could be lost wandering these woods for life. I looked at the map again. This is where it ends and begins. I breath in and look at my dog.

"Hey buddy, you ready to join me?"

Midnight barked, I picked the trail on my right, tied my first ribbon to a branch. I pulled out my blade, and with the gun on my back I started to cut an old trail that needed to be marked again. We got a little ways down the trail, being careful to keep marking my progress with the ribbon. With Midnight by my side we keep going. By my watch and by the position of the sun in the sky I knew it was about twelve. I looked behind me where the ribbons fluttered in the light breeze. I'd made a lot of headway on the trail. I decided to take a break, I cleared a spot and made a small fire then I pulled out the dried meat and Bannock and started eating. Nearby a branch broke with a crack, loud in the silence. The dog jumped into defense mode, barking wildly at the bush. I pulled the gun from my back, flipped the safety off, and pointed it toward the spot Midnight was focused on. I took a deep breath, my eyes never leaving the bush. I took another deep breath to ease the pounding of my heart. For a moment I closed my eyes and sought to find the calm at my center. Midnight grew more agitated and leaped into the woods. It was so thick and dense I couldn't see through the branches. I whistled and called for him. The sound of him crashing through the bush on his return sent relief coursing through me. Rabbits ! That's what I heard. I put my gun down slowly and looked around. Time to move on and find a camping spot for the night. Dog by my side, I packed up and started on the trail again. Sometime later, a strange tingling ran over my skin, like ants or flies crawling on bare flesh. It spooked me. Someone or something was watching me. I kept walking, telling myself it was only my imagination. Eventually, the feeling passed.

The air took on a chill, I glanced up at the sun and checked my mental calculations with my watch. Three in the afternoon. I could go on but decided to make camp instead. I went further along the trail searching for a good place to spend the night. To my surprise and consternation, the trail forked at a place with a small clearing. There wasn't any mention of this fork on my maps. None of the elders said anything about another fork. I decided to stay here for the night and figure out what to do in the morning.

I cleared a spot for my tent and started to set up camp. The dog was on edge, just like me, looking around. I gave him water and he sat close to me. The tent was up and now I needed to gather some wood for the fire. I placed a ribbon on the tree next to me then strapped the gun to my side and started gathering dead falls and twigs. Once I had enough I started the fire and made sure it was caught. I looked at the sun, it was going down behind the trees. Time to get the night gear on. I unrolled the sleeping bag, dug out the parka, and threw more wood on the fire. Then I zipped up the tent, had a bite with the dog, and started drawing out which way I took on the map. I looked at my compass and wrote it all out, then replaced things in the pack and set the gun by my side. I had just got comfy, all tucked in and warm, ready for my book when Midnight's ears perked up and he jumped upright, giving a low growl. I sat up, heart thumping.

"What is it?" I whispered.

He growled again. Taking the gun I unzipped the tent and peered into the dark. I stepped out and looked around. I slipped the safety off and was ready for anything. There was cracking in the trees and a faint wind blowing the leaves. I stood there a few minutes, nothing but old dead trees leaning against each other. The creaking noise almost sounded like breaking trees. I backed up and looked around. Without taking my eyes off the trees, I reached down and threw two big logs on the fire. Then, I sat on the frozen tree stump sticking out of the ground, and just listened for a bit. Nothing. Maybe I'm just over tired and paranoid. I have never been this deep in the mountains before without my grandparents. I straightened my spine and realized that I must overcome my fear. I crawled back in my tent with Midnight and finally fell into an exhausted sleep.

Everything seemed so real, I was sure I must be awake, but somehow transported back to when I was very young. I remember I always had these odd dreams but when I woke up I could never recall what they were about, only that they were important. Grampa said I would remember when the time was right, when I needed to remember. SO, I guess he was right, because now, I remember the dream and I am living it again.

* * *

I was only 6 years old. I was running down a trail, towards the sound of water. As I crested the hill, I was standing in front of a beautiful waterfall, with the sun shining down making sparkles like diamonds all over the top of the water. A peaceful, breathtaking place. I am walking toward it, and Midnight is with me, I feel happy with no fear, only a relaxing peace. I step into the water and the sky suddenly turns dark, thunder and lightning crashes through the sky. My heart thunders in my chest and it's hard to breathe. There standing above the waterfall is a woman screaming and pointing at me, the waterfall's water turns to blood, my heart jumps in triple time, and I am running wildly in the woods scared and terrified.

I come fully suddenly awake, dripping with sweat and freezing. A small cry escapes my lips. I want my grandma. Midnight opened his eyes and looked up at me. I shook my head and wiped the tears away with the back of my hand. I drank some water and tried to order my thoughts. Why am I having a weird dream? Is this something I am supposed to remember. Am I, as some say, losing my mind? Nah. It's just something important that I need to remember. It may come in useful in the coming days. I lay back down, prayed, and went back to sleep with Midnight close by my side.

Chapter Three

Morning ~ Day 3

The Sun was up. I looked at my watch. Eleven-thirty! How did I sleep through the alarm? Ugh! I jumped up and then I started to panic a bit. I had to stay on track if I expected to make it to my destination and back. I checked the fire and discovered it had burned out during the night. Grampa would shake his head in disgust at me. I woke flames from the ashes then made coffee, had a quick bite, and packed up. I had planned out my route with such care and I was annoyed that I'd lost 4 ½ hours by missing the alarm. I only had half a day till sundown. I shouldered the pack, tied my ribbon to a bush and headed out.

Midnight was just ahead of me when I started to get that eerie feeling again that someone was watching me. I kept my cool, outwardly giving the impression I was unaware of their scrutiny. I kept cutting back the bushes that were too thick to pass through. After I'd gone a small way I stopped in frustration. The trail seemed to have gotten bushier and more overgrown. It was going to take me all day to get even a short way through this section. I threw my pack down and looked at the map, I was quite a ways from where I'd initially started, but the going was increasingly difficult. I sat for a minute to catch my breath and organize my thoughts. Midnight had wandered off chasing a rabbit. I pulled out my compass to mark my map.

Branches rattled and broke in the near distance. I looked but didn't see anything, Probably the silly dog chasing rabbits. I relaxed and let my guard down feeling oddly tired. I packed the map and tied another marker by the side of the trail. I whistled for Midnight and waited for him to bound out of the bush. Nothing... Where the heck was that darn dog? Leaves rustled, then a branch snapped...that wasn't Midnight. Suddenly, alert, I reached for my gun and flicked it under my arm. Throwing the safety off, I knelt on the ground and turned a full circle. Whatever was out there was coming closer. My heart pounded as I wished Midnight was with me. All the 'I should have's' popped in my head, all kinds of 'what if's'. Why did I let my guard down even a bit? Clear as day, my grandpa's voice told me to breathe and listen, to let nature speak. I took a deep breath and slowed my heart. The noise got closer, the leaves and small twigs breaking were now within six feet to the north of where I knelt.

I stayed quiet and remained calm. Out of the thickest of the brush stepped the biggest, beautiful, white as the snow, deer I had ever laid my eyes on. The eyes were red as the blood running through my body. I gasped and put my gun down. I stared in disbelief. Was this really happening to me? There were stories told of spiritual animals that lived in these mountains who could grant you a safe passage through your journeys. The deer stepped out on the trail I had been working on, regarded me with solemn eyes, then looked around. I prayed that I had not offended him by cutting the path. My gaze followed him as he walked past me calmly, so big and wise, with his head held high as though to tell me it was okay, and I was safe.

I kept my head down, not meeting his eyes, as he walked past me. His very presence gave me the biggest boost of confidence and courage I had ever felt. I continued to watch him from under my lowered lids as he disappeared into the trees down the path.

Another sound startled me, and I grabbed the gun. Midnight burst out of the undergrowth with the rabbit he'd been chasing in his mouth. I let out a breath of relief and looked at him as if to say "Really?" He dropped the rabbit and gave me that look, a look I knew all too well, it was the 'I'm hungry' look. A quick glance at my wrist revealed the time was now 3:10pm, I had spent four hours breaking trail. It was time to make camp for the night. I dug in my pack and pulled out a piece of dried meat. I bit off a chunk and shared some with Midnight.

Third Night

I began to unpack the tent and gear for the night, as I tugged on my parka a small moose hide bag fell out. Surprised, I looked inside and realized my uncle had also packed me some sage. I smiled. He did care. I was getting used to setting up the tent by now as I'd done it so often, it popped open easier. I unrolled my bag and threw my pack in. I tied the rabbit high in the tree then Midnight and I started looking for deadfall. We didn't have to go far before I found a pile of dead wood and carried an arm full back to the camp site. I went back for more with Midnight on my heels, watching my back. I soon had a nice pile of wood that should last the night, so I started on a dug out for the firepit area. After that work my body ached with weakness. I gave Midnight a look that said, "Well buddy, I think we need to take a day off tomorrow and gather our strength for the next few days." Midnight lifted his paw and put it on my hand as though to tell me he agreed with my decision to rest.

I started a fire and skinned the rabbit, then wrapped all the remains for after we ate. The smell and the sound of fresh firewood burning was a comfort. The popping and crackle of the fire was soothing. The sparks spiraling upward in the cooling air looked like little lights flashing in the dark. I grabbed my pack from the tent and brought out my knife with the blade wrapped in soft leather for safety. Midnight stood watching while I sharpened a stick to spit the rabbit on. It slid through the meat nicely as I set it up over the flames. I pulled the dried herbs Grandma sent along. I had a lot of dried meat and Bannock to last me at least two weeks. There were also 8 potatoes, 8 carrots, and 3 onions which was wonderful for flavoring. And last, but not least, tea bags, and coffee, sugar, and creamer for my mix. Grandma always knew what to pack for long hikes and journeys. I flipped the rabbit, then started to cut up one potato and a carrot. I added a couple of fresh mushrooms I'd picked off the land, pulled the tin foil out and steamed my veggies with my herbs. The aroma was tantalizing and made Midnight whine and drool. I laughed at him and pulled up a log to sit on. Pouring a small tin pot full of water, I placed it down for Midnight. He was thirsty, and I started to wonder if maybe, there was a spring nearby to collect some fresh water. I planned for long days once we were back on the trail.

The rabbit was done, I pulled the stake out of the ground and scooped the tin out from the side of the fire. Everything smelled delicious. I had already placed my tin plate ready. Midnight whined, I laughed at him and leaned over to give him a hug. I love that dog. I ripped the rabbit in pieces and gave him his share. The carrots were so tender mixed in the herbs and mashed potatoes . Dinner was amazing. Midnight and I both ate and I made sure we had nothing lingering around the camp site as I cleaned up. Midnight was on guard, him and I went for a walk as far west from our site as we could to bury the entrails of the rabbit. I marked our trail as we went, keeping my eyes on the moon and stars to help guide us back to my fire.

I dug a small hole in the damp ground and put the rabbit's remains in it. I covered it well as Midnight stood close on guard.

A weeping woman's voice cried out in the dark. I froze, and a cold sweat poured over me. I looked around, my hand buried in the dog's scruff. Midnight growled, ears in the air and tail straight up. He was scared too. I turned and started back, rushing as fast as my feet could go. I wanted to run, but didn't want whatever it was out there to guess how scared I was. I kept my eyes on the moon and stars as guide. I could see my fire glowing in the distance, I hurried toward it and before I knew it, I was running, heart pounding so hard my chest vibrated with every beat. Midnight ran beside me. A small whine passed my lips as I reached my fire and threw myself into the tent. I used to do that when I was a child and something scared me. I wished my grandpa was there to protect me. Midnight barked and growled outside by the fire and that heightened my fear. I held the gun close and took a deep breath. I was alone in the woods with only the Creator knew what was out there wailing. I kept in mind why I was on this journey, reminding myself it was my choice to be here to prove to my grandparents I was all grown up. Fear turned into courage as I wiped my tears and stepped out of the tent. I was ready to face whatever showed up and protect Midnight. I calmed my dog down, with the gun in my hand I looked and listened. My heart still pounded, I took another deep breath and let it out releasing the fear that was left. My heart calmed, and now I could hear an owl deep in the bush. Another deep breath, I held this one for a second, as I closed my eyes. Midnight calmed down but was aware and alert to our surroundings. The fire crackled once again. I could hear Midnight panting. He decided it was time to go to bed, so he relaxed his stance and hopped into the tent. I worked on calming myself, sitting quietly and listening. Then I threw more logs on the fire making it two feet high so it was bright enough that I could see any shadows creeping up on us. The moon gave off a bright glow in the sky, the cold and slight frost in the air settled in. I decided it was time to call it a night, since the lack of rest was making me hear things that weren't there. Midnight was already in the tent watching. I crawled in and zipped up the flap. It was warmer inside. I flipped on the small flashlight I kept on my key holder. It was comforting to push the dark back. I took the tissue out and looked at Midnight.

"I must go out again, buddy. Want to help me mark our camp?"

He barked then jumped up. I laughed and felt safe knowing he was with me. I opened the tent and stepped out. It was starting to get cold fast, quickly I went to the bathroom and put more logs on the fire then jumped back into the tent. Midnight dove in behind me. He loved to play around for a spot in bed the crazy dog. I giggled as I pushed him back to zip up the tent then crawled into bed. After half hour of listening for any weird noises, I fell asleep to the sounds of the fire and a hooting owl.

Second Dream

I had slipped into a deep sleep and in my dream I was in a hut. I looked around, there were herbs hanging all over and there was a shelf under a window opening with a bowl and stones. I turned my head to the left where there was a fireplace of rocks with a pot over the flames. Next to it was a small log carved into a seat with fur covering, to the right of that, was a small bed, big enough to fit two people. The ground under my feet was warm, and behind me was a door made of wood, with a small window beside it that had a fur hanging over one side of it. Rabbits hung on hooks by the door. I smelled soup, and I could see there was rabbit soup in the boiling pot. In the center was a table with two small log seats. I heard crickets singing and a crow squawking. I looked at my hands as I reached for the door. They were the hands of a young woman. I looked in a large bowl of water on the side of the table. The reflection was not of my own but showed a beautiful young native woman. My belly was heavy with child. What is this?

Chapter Four

Day Four

The insistent call of my alarm dragged me from sleep. What a dream. I rolled over, surprised to see the tent flap was left open. Outside, the birds were up and singing loudly. A soft breeze rustled the leaves as they gossiped with each other. It looked like it must be a nice day. I zipped the flap back up and reset the alarm for 10:am and curled back into my bedroll. The alarm startled me awake at the appointed time. I got up and stretched my muscles, feeling better for the rest after all the bushwhacking I'd done the day before. I opened the tent and Midnight ran out. I crawled out after him and took a deep breath. Now, I felt awake. I checked my pack and pulled out the pot and water bottle. Midnight whined for a drink, so I poured some into the pot for him. I set about lighting the fire and starting my coffee. The sun was hot and bright. I love the spring mornings when everything is so fresh and beautiful.

The water over the fire was boiling so I put my coffee grounds in, let it brew, and poured a cup. I sat back, took out a smoke, then started thinking about the night before and the dream. I pulled my pack over and took out my notes of the elders' stories I had recorded for this journey.

As the story was told by elders: There was a beautiful woman that lived alone on the outskirts of the village, and she was a healer. The hunters in the village would fight over who would be her suitor. But as time went by, the chief still did not approve any man of the village to be her suitor. The chief believed the woman was a witch, one who had not aged a day past twenty. He banished her to the dark deep woods to roam endlessly with no people of her own, and her unborn child was killed because it was believed to be as evil as the woman who bore it.

She wept, as the women of the village threw rocks, forcing her to leave the village and the safety it offered. She stood at the edge of the tree line and cursed them, including all the generations of their bloodline to come after them. Then she disappeared into the forest.

A great sadness swept through me as I read the stories. Each one included the same warning. They all agreed, in one form or another, that the woman was still in these mountains. She haunted hunters and travelers and tormented them to the point where they lost their minds.

Was that her I heard in the night? Chills danced down my spine and raised the hairs on my arms. I shrugged and shook off the thought. That was just crazy thinking. It was just my hyper imagination because I was over tired. Maybe I was suffering from a lack of oxygen, being high up in the mountains? I shook my head, popped open a can of beans and ate that with some Bannock. I shared it with Midnight. Then, I made a few notes about my experiences so far.

I got to my feet. Time to go exploring. I took a small pack, with my parka just in case, and a few other things I might need. After I zipped up the tent, and marked my area with ribbons, Midnight and I headed out looking for water. I followed the trail higher. About twenty yards later, I walked into a huge open clearing. It was wide with tall golden straw like grass, on the other side were tall dark trees that cast a line of shadow all around. My stomach knotted with uneasiness. The place was spooky. Midnight was sharp on alert at my side. I tied a ribbon on the tree where I entered the clearing and kept adding them as I went across the open space, tying them to the long grasses. It was comforting to see that every twenty feet there was a bright orange ribbon waving in the wind, an orange line of safety through the yellow grass. I made it past the clearing and arrived at the edge of the shadows. In front of me was a women's hair ribbon tangled in the thorns. Midnight started barking and when I looked at him I saw he was actually standing by the beginning of a trail. I tied a ribbon to the tree at the entrance. The trail was a little overgrown with bush, but it was obviously well used, and I wondered by who or what.

I stopped and listened for a second. The world felt strange, I could hear rushing water, birds, and the dead leaves rustling in the soft breeze. Somewhere a crow squawked, but beneath the other sounds of nature going about her business, there was silence. Midnight had calmed down, so I felt okay with moving forward.

The sun was still high enough for me to get back to camp by night fall. The trail was narrow, black dirt packed down as though it had been walked on many times. Through the trees, I could see small patches of purple flowers. Beside the trail were herbs of all sorts. At first glance it was like I had walked into another season of the year. Breathtaking lush green moss grew everywhere, the air was moist and humid, huge trees with roots sprawling all over the place lined the path. The branches overhead touched each other creating an arched walkway over the trail. The sunbeams slanted through the trees like strips of lights marking the way. It was beautiful and breathtaking. As I walked closer to the end, I tied another ribbon to a tree. At the end of the trail vines hung like a curtain. I pushed through, and no more than 25 feet from me to the right was the waterfall from my dream.

Shock held me immobile, and fear skittered over my skin. I dreamed it, and yet it was real. How could that be? Just like in the dream, Midnight was by my side. It must be another dream. Yup, I should wake up soon. To test that theory, I pinched my arm.

"Ouch!"

This was not a dream. Midnight seemed unconcerned, drinking his fill from the pool by the falls. I looked around and realized that the trail continued along both sides of the creek and up into mountain sides. I filled my water container and called for Midnight. Leaving the falls behind, I followed the right side of the trail. After 15 minutes or so, the rocky trail headed into a creepy dark forest. I glanced at my dog, Midnight's hackles were standing, his tail and ears up. A low growling vibrated from his throat, his teeth glistening in the dim light. His wild barking set me on edge. I pulled out my gun and pointed it toward the trees.

"What is it, boy? What's there?"

I slipped the safety off, and swung the gun toward the direction Midnight was facing. I knelt and stayed still. Midnight ran back and forth, trying to get closer to where the trail entered the woods.

Then, I heard it again. A woman weeping in the forest. My heart kicked in my chest. Drumming echoed in my breastbone, getting louder and louder. The drumming came closer and closer through the trees. I couldn't run, my feet refused to move, as thoughts raced through my head. The drumming was closer now, coming from nowhere and everywhere at once. Hemming me in. I want so bad to run, but my muscles won't answer my commands.

Midnight kept barking, running around me. The sound was so loud I jammed my hands over my ears, the gun in the crook of my arm. I closed my eyes against the pain. When I opened them again Midnight was on the ground, not moving. I tried to scream, but nothing came out. Even if I did scream as loud as I could, the drumming would drown it out. Black started to creep in from the sides of my vision, the ground came up to meet my face. Or did I just fall down?

* * *

Somewhere there is a loud crowd of people.; I looked out the window. Where did the window come from? Where am I? Where is Midnight. My body trembles with fear. A group of women are approaching the hut led by a man with a staff. I yank open the door, my voice trembling and vibrating. "What do you want here?"

The large man reaches my hut, pushes his way through, knocking me down as he yells at me. Accusing me of being a witch, claiming that I am with a child of evil origin. I beg and plead with this man, telling him his son is the father of the child I am carrying.

He reared back, ready to strike out at me. "You lying witch! You lie like the snake that feeds off the innocents!" Spittle foams on his lips. "I'm done with you," he shrieks and sweeps out.

In his wake, two big women grab me, holding my arms tight. They are so big, and I am small and weak compared to them. They drag me outside, spin me around and force me to watch them burn my hut to the ground with everything I own still inside. My cries and wails go unheeded.

"You are banished to walk the trees as a witch. You are never to set foot in the village again," the man with the staff decrees in a loud voice.

My two captors, along with a few others force me to the edge of the valley, through the trees, down the trail by the waterfalls, far from the village. Once there, they proceed to hit and kick me as I fall, screaming for mercy for my child. Through the kicking legs, I see the love of my heart, my child's father, and I reach out, crying for him to come and save us.

He averted his eyes, turned and walked away. I died inside and gave up the fight for my own life and that of my child. I closed my eyes after the women were done abusing me, leaving me there to die.

There was a growling of thunder as I crawled to the waterfall. I collapsed in the shallows and drank a handful of water. I was numb, there was pain, but it did not seem to be mine. I was covered in blood; my child was gone. Pain pierced the numbness clouding my mind, and I screamed as loud as I could. My voice broke and my throat bled. My hands are submerged in the water, above them is my battered reflection, eyes dark with shock and pain. A crow squawked beside me,, our eyes met, and my pain turned to anger. Revenge blackened my shadow, my soul offered itself to the darkness. I am transformed and vowed they would all pay for what they had done. No matter how long it took.

* * *

My head spun and the ringing in my ears was deafening. My body refused to obey me. My struggle to get up only resulted in my arms flopping, my vision was blurred, and my voice didn't seem to be working. What happened? What is going on? Where is Midnight? Am I dead?

A faint rattling sound catches my attention. A muffled low sound emerges from my mouth.

"Get up, you must get up. It's not safe to stay here," Grampa's voice urges me.

Is he here? How can he be here? I manage to move a bit. It felt like the time my friends and I drank something we shouldn't have. I blinked a few times, the sky was still blurry, blue black with every blink. Midnight's head came into my line of sight, licking my face repeatedly. When I responded he gave a happy whine.

Finally, I could move my arms and legs. My vision returned, stars and moonlight shone down on me. How long did I lie there? Rocks poked into my back, and it was cold. I shivered and rolled over. Owls hooted in the trees and crickets sang in the grasses by the trail. A wind blew in the trees. My feet were wet, how strange that I was wet. Midnight barked at me in the dark, urging me to get up and get going.

I was by the stream or creek that ran off the mountain. It was too dark and the entrance to the trail was obscured by the shadows. There was no way I would make it back to my camp tonight. I walked back the way I had come, Midnight by me. I reached the falls and followed the trail that led to the other side. It was hard going in the faint light. I tied a ribbon to the bush by the falls. Just past the bushes was a clearing with a couple of old half-falling down huts. There must have been a village here at one time. Midnight and I walked through the tall grass to the far side of the clearing. My footsteps bending the grass in my wake. I took out my flashlight and swung the beam back and forth. There wasn't much to see. The wind rattled the tree branches and ruffled the grasses. I needed to find a safe place for my fire and also some shelter from the wind. I found one hut with a small waist-high wall still standing. It would have been perfect except the wind came from the wrong side.

Midnight barked and ran to another crumbled building. I stumbled across to it, half the hut was standing, and the wind was outside it. I dropped the pack pulled the parka out and put it on. The wind had a sharp edge, and I was freezing. Starting a fire was my priority. With the gun in the crook of my arm I searched the area nearby and soon had an armful of sticks and deadfall. My legs ached and fatigue dragged at me. I threw the firewood down and dropped to my knees. I tucked my feet under me in an effort to warm them up. I took my knife out of the pack and started digging a spot in the ground for my fire pit. Once I had the hole ready, I threw in leaves along with a dry grass bundle. Using one of my matches, I started the tinder on fire and built it up with little dry twigs and sticks before adding some larger pieces. As the fire grew it threw enough light for me to see my surroundings. The heat warmed my hands and my soul.

Midnight sat close to the fire, looking as cold as I felt in spite of his fur coat. I brought out the leftover rabbit leg with the potatoes and herbs from my pack. I heated it in the coals and then ate half, sharing the rest with my dog. It would have to do until we made it back to camp in the morning.

I threw more wood on the flames. In the corner of the hut, buried in the clay, I found an old pottery bowl. I filled it with water for Midnight. I ventured away from the fire to cut down some bushes and hauled them back to the hut. I explored a little more with the small key chain flashlight that was hardly giving off any light. My moccasins were stiff, and I couldn't feel my feet properly. I needed to gather more brush to make a bed and a bit of a better shelter or Midnight and I would both be covered with frost by morning.

I cut more bushes and hauled them back. I rested for a moment before I mustered up the energy to go and look for anything else that might be helpful. Midnight came with me when I left the ring of firelight. From the darkness came what sounded like a group of people talking.

* * *

I stopped just outside the light of my fire. Who was out there and how could there be anyone? I knew very well that the surrounding area was empty. So, what was going on? A little way away a fire flickered in the night. Three men sat in the fire's light. It was their voices I was hearing. I rubbed my eyes. Was I so tired and cold I was imagining things? Midnight's ears perked up and he went into guard mode, a low growl rumbling in his chest. With my hand buried in his neck fur we walked towards them. I lifted my arm and called to them.

"Hello?" I kept walking. "Hello, can I join your fire?

They stood up and turned toward me in silence. One of them pulled a bow from his back and an arrow from a quiver.

I stopped and held my hands up. "Whoa, stop!"

Midnight jumped in front of me barking aggressively.

The older man yelled at the others to calm down. The men listened to the old guy and backed off, I yelled at Midnight to stop, and everything calmed down.

After the others settled down, the old man spoke. "I am Albert. Come set by the fire and warm yourself up."

One of the men offered me his seat. I nodded my thanks and sat down. Another of the men offered me hot tea.

Albert smiled and regarded me thoughtfully. "What are you doing up in these mountains? You shouldn't be here. I am the guardian and spirit guide of these mountains. What is your journey? Explain yourself."

I cleared my throat. "I am on a journey to seek out the medicine woman who the stories say is able to heal the sick. She knows the herbs that are hidden in these mountains."

The men regarded me in shock, hisses of disbelief passing their lips.

"Those who search for unspoken women and the legends of such medicine must pay the price for what they seek. For those that seek truth; it's wisdom and knowledge. For others that seek the women and the medicine; it's a journey that never ends. You will be lost in the forest of your own mind searching forever." Albert's eyes held me still, unable to move or speak.

A silence settled over the clearing.

Finally, Albert spoke, breaking the spell of silence. "The choice is always a journey that one must make for themselves, and the path must be chosen wisely." The old man released me from his gaze.

I drank my tea then stood up. The men stood up as well. It seemed they were preparing to bid me farewell. Albert petted Midnight and gave him a hide. He nodded to a younger man who dug out a small, well wrapped hide bag, along with a large hide rolled up as a blanket which he handed to me.

I smiled at them. "Thank you for the gifts, I wish I had something to give in return."

Albert laughed. "You remind me of someone I knew long ago."

Midnight barked and trotted off toward the fire by the ruined hut. I turned to wave farewell to the old man and his followers. My heart jumped in my chest. Only darkness greeted me, there was no fire and the men were gone.

Unable to believe my eyes, I ran back to the clearing. Nothing. No sign that anyone had ever been there, no ashes or coals, not even a fire pit. I stared at Midnight who looked up at me, head tipped to the side.

What just happened? Was the whole thing some weird illusion or trick of my mind? Was it real?

I looked down at the contents of my hands. It must have been real. I have the hides that the men gave me. Were they spirits? Who were they? I wished Grampa was here to help me make sense of this.

I shook my head and headed back to my fire, hoping it was still burning. When I reached the hut, the fire was burning low, but still emitting some heat and light. I added more wood, and by the increased light, I laid out the bushes I had cut earlier. I piled the bigger ones with more branches in the corner of the old hut and created a side wall to make a tent like shelter. I grinned, it reminded me of the little forts we used to make as kids in the woods. It was just big enough for me and Midnight. I piled more brush over the top and kept the fire going. It was actually warm and cozy in the corner of the hut.

I used my pack as a pillow and laid down with Midnight snuggled in beside me. I threw the rolled up hide over us. It was thick and heavy enough to cover us both and keep us warm. I lay on my side and watched the fire dancing until I fell asleep.

* * *

I opened my eyes surrounded by thick smoky fog. Somewhere nearby I heard my grandma singing. I knew I must be dreaming but started walking forward through the fog anyway, curious to see where it would lead me. The fog thinned and I could see a fire ahead of me. I walked towards it and to my surprise I found the three men who had gifted me with the hide.

I was relieved and happy to see them.

"Hello," I called, entering the circle of firelight.

Albert got to his feet with a smile on his weathered face. So, you made it here as well. We have been waiting for you."

I didn't quite understand what he meant. Where was here? I smiled and accepted the tea he pressed into my hands. I sat by his fire and this time he was more forthcoming.

"If your journey has led you to us, you must be a seeker of the truth. Are you ready for your own journey?"

"I am, but I have questions that need answers," I replied.

He smiled. "You ask the right questions. You get good answers."

I nodded and we sipped our tea in silence.

I broke the silence. "Who is the woman in my dreams?"

Albert looked grave. "She is but an angry lost soul that hunts. She seeks revenge on the descendants of those who took so much from her. When someone hears her weeping, it means she has found a person of the cursed bloodline."

I forced the tea down past the hard lump in my chest and cleared my throat.

"If a person hears her weeping, what happens to them and how does a person make her go away?"

He looked at me seriously and got to his feet. "It is time for you to find your answers." He walked off into the night followed by his silent companions.

I turned around and found myself in a village full of people. Little kids running around, elderly women sitting around laughing and talking. In the midst of the activity, I recognized a familiar face. My great, great grandfather. He approached me and shook my hand.

"You must have come from afar to find me, only a few have ever made it this far to tell the tale, but your journey has just begun my great granddaughter."

My lips moved but no sound came out. He knows me! How can he know me when he has never met me?

"Come we must prepare." He gestured and I followed him into another thick fog bank. I stepped through the mists, and he stopped me with his hand.

"Look," he said and pointed to a path leading into a green clearing.

A woman stood there, dressed in earthy tones with matted grey hair. Twigs, leaves, and grass clung all over her. Everything about her was grey. Standing beside her was a young girl around seven years old. The older woman was teaching her how to bring wind and rain. The woman waved her arms in the air in a circle and the sky started to darken. The clouds followed the direction of her arms.

I woke up with a start, sitting upright in my bedroll. Midnight grumbled and gave me a reproachful look for waking him up too.

Chapter Five

Day Five
　　I checked the time when I woke up: 6:35am. What was going on with these weird dreams I kept having? I needed to clear my head, so I got up. I pulled my parka on and looked at Midnight.
　　"You coming or staying in bed?"
　　He grunted and put his paws over his eyes and face.
　　"It's cool, stay in bed I don't mind." I laughed at him as I rolled over to get out of my bush tent. The hide was so warm, it had helped a lot through the cold night. I started the fire, sat down, and watched the flames get a little bigger. I grabbed my little pot to make coffee out of my pack, glad I still had coffee. I smiled to myself, lost in thought, I started to think about everything. I had a cup of coffee and decided to meditate while the sun was still rising. I dragged the hide out of the hut, laid it by the fire and sat on it. I dug out the hide bag that was a gift from my elders, the sage that was packed by my uncle, then took a pinch of tobacco. I knelt and prayed as I did my offerings to the Creator for answers and guidance. I sat still as I

breathed deeply and let my body float. I could feel my soul lifting as the trance deepened.

There was a raven by the little girl's side laying on the ground, lifeless. The old woman and the little girl picked it up, both whispered something to it. The bird moved and squawked, flapped its wings, and flew to a log. They brought the bird back to life, how I wished I knew the secret of doing that. Even in trance, my heart skipped a beat.

The scene faded into another. The old woman walked through the forest, just the other side of the mountain, teaching the little girl all about herbs and berries, leaves and moss, rotten trees, and the healing of them, picking flowers. The voices became loud enough for me to hear them. The old woman spoke to the little girl. "These purple flowers only grow here in this part of the mountain, and nowhere else. If crushed down and boiled they can cure the sick of all kinds of sickness, but it will only grow once every two years. It is rare to find it, and only a few have knowledge of this flower."

I came back to myself, confused and angry. I didn't get any answers, only dreams and visions of spirits. Things I didn't understand the meaning of and that left me with more questions than answers. Doubt reared its head. Am I still too young for this? Should I turn back? Go home without the cure I was looking for?

A dead tree crashed to the ground in the forest, bringing me to my feet, gun in hand. Midnight was barking and jumping all over the place. I look toward the forest, signaling Midnight to be quiet. I could detect no sound, just the thunder of waterfalls in the distance. Midnight wasn't scared, just alert.

I took a breath and looked at the time: 8:30am. I needed to find myself something to eat. The vision quest exhausted me. I went back to my fire. It had burned down, so I put a couple of logs on it, crawled back in the bush tent and laid down.

I must have fallen asleep. Midnight's barking woke me. I grabbed my gun and crawled out of the hut. The dog barked and looked down. On the ground at my feet were two fresh rabbits, still warm. He must have gone hunting while I crashed. I laughed and hugged him.

"Yeah boy, let's eat. I'm starving"

Midnight barked and curveted around. I checked the time: 10:am.

"Not bad. Good boy." I started to skin the rabbits. Once they were clean, I skewered them and got the stakes in the ground with the rabbits ready to cook over the fire.

I laid back on the hide with Midnight curled up by me. I was so proud of him. I stroked his face and gave him kisses. He turned on his back like a big puppy to get his belly rubs. I love that dog.

I loved where we had camped. I marked the place on the map. Everywhere we'd gone

I had marked my trail. As far as I could tell, this location was nowhere anyone had gone for a very long time. I was happy I had picked this direction to go in.

These trails must be hundreds of years old and who knew where others went before me in these mountains. I started recording my notes of the journey so far in my diary. Peace filled my heart. The area was full of beautiful landscapes. I loved it here. I just wanted to set up camp and stay forever.

Maybe I could make this place my summer camp. I breathed in the piney mountain air. The cooking rabbits made my stomach growl. Midnight was waiting for his share, a thin line of drool shining on his muzzle.

I pulled the rabbits from the fire and laid them on the side before pulling out the herbs I wanted to add. I made our tin foil plates, and we ate in happy silence. Midnight and I were both satisfied, and I thanked the Creator for this day.

After taking care of the remains and any trash we'd made, I decided to take a walk and see what else was around. If this was the old village in the stories, there must be a trail around here somewhere that led to her hut. I looked at my watch and checked the angle of the sun: 11:45am. I had time to explore before the sun set again. Midnight and I headed towards the dark edge of the clearing. We explored the edge and found nothing. No trails, no markings, no nothing.

I looked at my map, I had to make my own as I went, since this was new territory and all. I walked all around the edge. Far back, behind a thick bush, there was something of a trail. I wasn't sure if it was a trail or just an animal path but decided to explore. I tied off a ribbon and headed in with Midnight on my heels. I pushed through the thick undergrowth. It didn't thin out at all, so I tied more ribbons as I went. The trail went back further than I could see, and I was getting a bit uneasy. I hadn't brought my pack with me, and I ran out of ribbons to mark the way back. I tied off the last one and headed back. I needed the rest of my gear. It was 3:pm when I got back to hut. I was excited to go check out that trail. I needed to go back to my base camp and get my tent and gear.

I called Midnight and headed toward the falls. Hoping to see, if by chance, I could find that other trail outside the falls that knocked me out and I met Albert for the first time. I was a bit scared, but I had to know if it was really there or if I imagined it.

We reached the falls. Midnight plunges his head in like he has been without water for days.

I laughed. "Slow down boy, or you'll choke." I bent down and filled my container of water then started walking towards the dark side of the falls and mountain. The air was moist, heavy, and damp. No sun reached this place and made it spooky with shadows.

I walked close and found the trail. I wasn't going crazy. I looked at my watch: 4:pm. It had taken an hour to get here. The feeling in my gut said I should turn back. I didn't mess with gut feelings.

Grandpa always told me to listen to that feeling. "It's your spirit's way of warning you that something is not right."

I dug in my pack and took out some tobacco. I left a bit there on the rocks and gave thanks before I started to walk back. A small pebble came flying out of the forest and hit the rocks behind me. I turned quickly.

"Who's out there?" My heart was pounding. There was no reply. I started running, Midnight beside me. My heart beating so fast I couldn't breathe. I stopped on the other side of the falls and looked back to see if there was anything after me. Nothing. I slowed my breathing and walked slowly back to the hut site.

Midnight had no clue what was happening. He panted along beside me, the look on his face made me laugh out loud. I put my hands on my knees and petted him.

"Did you see that, boy? Something, or someone, threw that rock at us."

I laughed harder, bordering on hysteria. I wished my uncle were here to see this. He would have laughed his guts out at me. I shook it off. It was quite the excitement, and probably some small animal just dislodged the pebble. I had never felt that rush of adrenalin before. It was wild. Still a little shaken up, I got a fire going. The sun was starting to set, and the damp cold started to slowly creep in. By the sun, it was 5:30 or so.

Thunder in the distance brought my attention back to the sky which had started to darken.

No! It's going to rain, and I have no real cover.

The hut we sheltered in the night before had no roof to protect us from the storm. Panic set in as the lighting flashed in the sky in the distance. The wind picked up, soughing in the branches and scattering leaves and twigs before it. I ran around looking for something to make a cover. I couldn't lose my fire and if I got wet it would be bad. I could get sick out here and nobody would find me in time.

I grabbed my things, cradling a few precious embers in a bit of bark, and called Midnight. We ran towards the falls. I was hoping there might be a cave to shelter in nearby. Midnight and I arrived at the falls. Drops of water pearled on my skin. I prayed it was just water from the falls and kept looking for shelter. Soon there was more water in the air and on my skin. No, it was raining.

The trees might offer us some cover, but I was afraid of the forest. With Midnight on my heels, we ran into the forest in spite of my misgivings. We followed the trail downward into a hole and found a hollow tree. Midnight and I went through the opening. The tree trunk and roots were huge, tangled in bunches that made a shelter. The interior was so big you could stand up and walk around. No rain got through and it was dry. Dark, but warm and sheltered. It was beautiful. I had never seen anything like this. I flicked my flashlight on and looked around. The rain rattled loudly overhead, coming down like a waterfall.

It washed the air clean and fresh, I took a deep breath through my nose and exhaled, the sharp scent of the huge cedar that sheltered us redolent in the confined space. It was a miracle how nature washed everything away and left the fresh clean air in its place. The fear I felt washed away with the rain. I was grateful for the shelter nature provided. Midnight barked; he was looking at something moving in the far corner of the hollow.

"What is it, boy?"

I took my gun out, flipped the safety off, and pointed it towards the shadows. My heart thundered louder than the storm, fear set my body trembling. Midnight barked again, adding growls this time. A fox came skulking out of the shadows, belly down, tail tucked between its legs, and whining like a puppy. I yelled for Midnight to stop and lowered the gun.

"It's okay little guy, don't be afraid." I pulled out a piece of rabbit we had leftover and threw it to him. Midnight whined, and I gave him a look. "Really? He's scared and starving, we ate today."

I dug in the pack and gave Midnight some meat to keep him quiet. The fox finished his piece and stayed on his side of the shelter. Midnight and I stayed close to the entrance. The dog kept up a low growling and I had to keep telling him to stop. It was warm in our shelter, and I didn't feel the need to use the coals I'd brought with me to make a fire. It might not have been such a good idea anyway, seeing as we were huddled in the heart of a giant cedar tree.

It got dark out, and the rain was still pouring. Through a break in the clouds, the moon shone so bright it lit up bits of the forest. I pulled out the hide and laid it down before I slipped on my parka. I fell asleep feeling safe knowing I had Midnight and now a fox to keep guard.

* * *

Somehow, I knew I was dreaming again. These dreams must be important, so I concentrated on what was happening.

I walked towards a village. There was a young girl, no older than ten years, carrying things in a basket. There was a boy with her, obviously interested in her. Perhaps they were friends, maybe he wanted something more as he was a few years older than her.

He smiled and gave her a flower; she smiled back.

Suddenly, a man appeared and grabbed the boy, pulling him away from the girl. They left the girl standing alone looking after them with a confused expression on her face. The boy looked back at her as if to say he would see her again. The girl waved a hand in goodbye.

The next thing I saw was the same girl and boy, playing in the forest chasing butterflies. The girl caught one in her hand and lifted her hand toward the boy. He looked at her and her hands as she opened them and let the butterfly go. Together, they watched it fly up and away. He reached for her hand and held it softly. He bent over as if to kiss it when a woman yelled in anger and fear. His mother grabbed him roughly and pulled him away, glaring at the girl. The boy looked back at the young girl, with despair in his eyes.

The girl ran away with tears in her eyes through the forest to a hut. I recognized that hut, it was the one Midnight and I sheltered in, but in much better repair. She burst through the door and ran to the old woman sitting by the fire. The girl flung herself at the older woman, crying. "Why do they hate us so much?"

The old woman replied softly, "Some people are scared of what they do not understand. We are healers and that scares them because they do not understand what it is we do."

The young girl dried her tears and looked up. "What is it that we do?"

The women turned her face away. "We pick herbs and heal the sick. We listen to nature and she provides for us. Mother Nature is our mother, and the Creator is our father. Together they are a powerful source of energy that can heal the sick and teach us the medicine to pass down to one another. One day you will have a daughter to pass this knowledge to as well. It is in our blood to do so." She paused, then looked at the girl with a touch of fear. "But beware, if you lean into the darkness of others, drink of their despair, revenge, and sorrow, you will become the darkness that feeds off the fear of others. That line must never be crossed."

The little girl nodded, fear in her eyes.

From where I was watching, I stepped on a branch that broke with a loud crack. What?

The old woman's head snapped up and she rushed toward me, so near I could have reached out and touched her. She looked around wildly. Maybe she couldn't see me?

"There is someone here show yourself!" She grabbed black ash from the fireplace and threw it at me.

* * *

My vision went black, and I woke up. Rubbing my eyes I sat up. How did she know I was there? Did she see me when she threw the ash? It was a dream. How could she interact with me? Confused, I had a drink of water and calmed my racing heart. Midnight was still sleeping, as was the little fox. I looked at the time: 4:30am. The rain had stopped. I decided to get a bit more sleep before the sun rose. It was still too dark to move yet. I laid back down and fell back to sleep.

Chapter Six

Day Six

I opened my eyes and pushed Midnight away, my face wet from him licking me. I looked at the time: 7:30 am.

"Sweet, thanks boy." I sat up. I looked for the fox but the place where it had been sleeping was empty. "At least it didn't attack us, eh boy?"

I grinned at Midnight as I threw things in the pack to head out. I touched the roots and thanked the tree for the shelter it had provided as we left. The sun was out when we stepped out of the hollow, bright beams slanting down through the trees with golden light.

I headed back to my campsite hoping my tent was still upright. Midnight whined and nudged my hand. "Sorry bud, no time to eat this morning. We need to get moving if we want to make it back to the tent."

He barked and followed, tail waving. I headed down the path where the bright orange flags were fluttering in the wind. We hurried along the trail and finally my red and white tent came into view. It was still standing and nothing looked like it had been disturbed in my absence. I packed up as quick as I could, and headed back to the trail, following the orange flags. It was 2:pm by the time I made it back to the falls. I was excited to set up my camp now that I had the rest of my gear.

Midnight was already gone hunting by the time I had the tent set up and made a fire. I settled down by the firepit.

I went through everything and got the camp organized. Then I pulled out the map and wrote down the route I took the day before. Next, I recorded my dreams in the diary so that my grandpa could read them when I got back, maybe help me understand some deeper insights into my journey.

I was almost done writing everything out when I missed my dog. Midnight had been gone a little over an hour, more than enough time for him to have caught his breakfast.

"Where is he? I hope he's okay."

"Midnight!" I yelled as loud as I could, then held my breath to listen. Nothing, no sound at all.

Now I was getting really worried for him. Where is my dog? I yelled again. "Midnight. Come boy!" Again, I listened, the only sound was the wind blowing the tree leaves. I walked closer to the edge of the falls.

"Midnight!"

The sound of his barking reached me, faint and far away. Relief swept through me. Thank goodness he was okay.

"Come here, boy!" I whistled to reinforce my call.

The crash and rustle of bushes told me he was running back toward me. He came around the side of the rocks with a wild chicken in his mouth, looking proud of himself.

"Good boy." I petted him and he let me take the bird from his mouth.

"Let's cook this up for you, my brave great hunter." I ruffled his fur as he walked beside me, tail wagging. Midnight ran ahead a bit and froze in his tracks with his ears up. He started to bark like something was wrong. I stopped and pulled my gun around into my hands.

I was close enough to see our camp site clearly. My heart stuttered in my chest. Holy crap, there was a bear sniffing around the tent.

I pointed the gun in the air and shot off two rounds. The echoes reverberated against the rock increasing the volume of the sound. The bear grunted and swung its head back and forth before loping into the bush, away from the camp.

After making sure the bear wasn't hanging around, I started to cook up the chicken for us. It was getting late. Once the chicken was done, Midnight and I shared the feast.

The moon rose so big and bright, the stars started to come out. Thousands of them showed themselves. I looked up and picked out the big dipper. I remember my grandma telling me stories when I was little about the stars. I laid there and watched the fire dance. The wood cracking turned into drumming in my head. The drums got clearer and I realized it was my grandpa singing. He was sending me his guidance and telling me he was watching over me.

A deep calm came over me and I blinked sleepily. I crawled into the tent and zipped it closed. I fell into a deep sleep.

Night Six

The fog was thick as I walked into the dark. "You must be very quiet here," something whispered in my ear. I shook my head and followed a path that brought me to a hut in the back woods. I recognized the place. I had visited her here before in dreams and visions.

I approached carefully, and this time the little girl was not so young. She was around twelve years old now, the old woman was still the same. She didn't appear to have aged at all. She was teaching the little girl a ritual. She had assembled a tub with mud and some herbs and candles. The old woman chanted something in her tongue as she disrobed. The girl stood, and just watched while the old woman submerged her whole body and head in the tub of mud. A few minutes later she rose and got out of the tub, covered in mud. She covered herself with a robe and walked past me through the trees to the falls.

As the water flowed over her body, it washed away all the old dead skin. What was revealed was smooth, young skin, her grey hair washed clean and was now a crown of long, jet black hair which fell down below her knees. The woman was beautiful, and young, no more than thirty years of age.

I was amazed at what had been revealed to me.

I woke up with hope in my heart. I was getting closer to finding the medicine we needed. I was getting closer; I could feel it.

Chapter Seven

Day Seven

I woke up early and made a quick breakfast. I packed what I thought I'd need for the day and headed out. It was 8am by the time we got back to the trail where we found shelter and the fox. The trail itself was neat, the path went under a huge overgrown root, vines or the loops of roots were covered in bright green moss that caught some sun from the tops of the trees. The light shone on a stone path that led into the mountain side and then up the mountain. There was a cave above me. Walking further up, I came across a grave. I paused in respect but had no clue who lay there.

I passed through to the trail that led up the mountain. It was steep and narrow, and I found it a hard trail to climb as it hadn't been used in a long while. Midnight barked from behind me.

"Stay," I told him. "You can't come this way, it's too dangerous."

I carefully navigated the passage, and a few steps brought me into a living space that looked to be deserted for hundreds of years. The only way out was the way I had come in.

I sat for a minute and just looked around. There was nothing that seemed to be important to my quest here. Disappointment settled heavy in my chest. I'd come all this way for nothing. I went back to where Midnight waited and set off back down the mountain side. It was getting late, but I made it back to the camp by 4:30pm. Questions kept buzzing in my head. Was that where the witch woman had lived? Was that her in the grave? But if that was her final resting place, who buried her and marked the grave site? I shook my head in confusion.

Practical things took over, I needed to make dinner and go to bed. I had another long day tomorrow. I crawled in the tent but couldn't sleep. A quick glance told me it was 7pm. I rolled over and closed my eyes, determined to sleep.

I knew it was another dream even as I realized I was at the falls. The woman and her child were there. A loud crash split the air. The woman leaped up, dragged on some clothes, took her child's hand ran with the child through the forest. The crashing noise got louder, and people's voices rose over it. The woman hid the girl in a hole in the ground by the trees, outside the hut I found earlier. She kissed her daughter and cautioned her not to make a sound. The woman ran back to the hut and barred the door. A group of raiders from further down the mountains attacked the hut, forced their way in and killed her. They raided the hut of everything they could carry and then disappeared back down the trail.

The little girl stayed in the hole by the tree till the sun came up. Tentatively, she crawled out and scuttled to the hut, throwing fearful glances at the trees in case the raiders were still about. She dropped to her knees by her mother's lifeless body and wept as she held her mom in her little arms. A look passed over her face that terrified me, her eyes turned black as night, then she fell back and passed out.

My dreaming self screamed, and I woke screaming in my tent, heart racing. Midnight was on his feet with his hackles raised. I sat up and wrapped my arms around my knees, mind awash with confusion and more questions than I had answers. Who was she? Who were those raiders? Where did they come from? My mind was too tired to figure anything out. Midnight had gone back to sleep, and I snuggled up to him and slept. Maybe in the morning things would be clearer.

Chapter Eight

Day Eight
The next morning, I lay in bed and slept until the sun was high in the sky. Midnight disappeared to get a drink or do whatever it was dogs did when they were on their own.

I wasn't feeling well, but Midnight knew where I was, and would come back when he was ready. I fell back to sleep. I really needed a day off from my quest.

* * *

The fog was back and thicker than ever. I walked through it and saw the hut that seemed to be in all my dreams. The woman was there, her black eyes looking at me. Then the scene shifted. There was a grave, I watched the girl as she buried her mother. A black raven croaked loudly, and the girl turned and looked at me.

I woke up in a sweat and pushed back my sleeping bag. I got out my map and my diary. I started writing, my hands trembled with excitement. I might have found the mother's burial site, and if what I saw in the dream was that woman's grave, was it the one I passed yesterday? It looked the same, as near as I could tell. The dreams are real, and they had a message for me. I was sure of it. I just needed to figure out exactly what they were trying to tell me.

By the time the sun was directly overhead I was feeling better. Mustering my energy, I grabbed some things including a change of clothes and socks. As the sun was warm, I decided to take a shower at the falls. I needed to refresh myself and get some food in me. I was ready for another adventure with Midnight. I headed to the falls, Midnight had returned and trotted by my side. He needed a wash down too.

I stripped down to my undies and walked into the water going to the deeper side. Midnight and I played, splashing around in the pool. I had a blast wrestling with him and in the end, he got his bath. All the dirt came off him and he looked like a new dog.

I ducked under the falls and let the water fall over my head and down my body. It was cold and refreshing, as I pulled my hair back to get all the water out, a sense of peace enveloped me. I was frozen through, so I hopped out and rushed into where the sun warmed the rocks. I dressed quickly in the clean clothes I had left there. Then, I washed my dirty clothes and wrung them out before spreading them on the hot rocks to dry a bit.

I brushed out my hair with my fingers. Midnight played with something in the water back by the falls. I braided my hair, which made me think of a time when my grandma used to brush my hair and braid it before bed. Midnight barked and jumped, pouncing on something in the water. I laughed at his silliness.

"What do you have there, you silly dog?" There was quite a bit of splashing, and I moved closer to see what he was playing with. "Is that a fish? No way!" I reached into the water and grabbed it before it could escape. I threw it as far back on the dry rocks as I could, snatched up a rock, rushed over, and smacked it,

"Good Boy. Look, boy. Lunch."

The dog jumped around me. I grabbed my damp clothes and started back to the tent. The birds were calling over the rush of the waterfall. Butterflies flitted in the bushes. squirrels chirped in the high branches jumping through the trees chasing one another.

Midnight was so much happier out here in the bush than he was in the village. Back home, the dogs were tied up all year long so that they didn't overpopulate or get into trouble. Midnight hates being tied up.

When we got back to the tent, I pulled out some fishing line and stretched it out, just enough to make a clothesline between two trees. I hung my clothes to dry. I stood back with my hands on my hips and surveyed my campsite; it was starting to feel like home here. I looked around for something to gut the fish on. I found a half of an old dead tree laying in the forested part of the clearing. I lifted it and a part broke off, almost like a board. I carried it back, but not too far. Midnight tagged along beside me while I searched for four tree sumps as equal in height as I could manage. I took them to where I had left the board.

I stopped for a drink of water and checked the time: 2:30. Midnight sat down with his tongue hanging out. I gave him a drink, and he was satisfied. I took the pack from the tent and pulled out what my uncle called "The Box".

I giggled at how silly that sounded. The Box was actually a travel kit containing a needle with some thread, band aids and ointment for wounds, safety pins, six nails, one small ball of string, glue, small scissors, rolled up snare wire, waterproof matches, two candles, a compass, and some bullets. He told me it contained everything I needed to survive in the wild.

I picked up the nails and grabbed a rock, then I nailed the board to the stumps., I stepped back to survey my work. I was so proud of myself that I did a little dance. Midnight danced with me. I dragged the heavy table towards the tree and decided that was where I would work. I made the fire and gutted the fish on the table, then spitted it over the fire to cook. I cut up the wild veggies I'd gathered, dug out the Bannock and the dried meat, and we had our own private feast--just me and Midnight. A look at my watch confirmed it was 4pm. I had really needed the rest and I was glad I'd taken the day off. My journey might end in just a few days, I realized. It didn't feel like I had been on the mountain for eight days but tomorrow would be day nine. Midnight was lying in the tent, content with his belly full. His fur was shiny and clean from the wash, he kept blinking, his eyes closing as he drifted into a doggy nap.

I sat soaking in the sun and thinking how beautiful this place was. Why hadn't anyone I knew ever been here? Or if they had, how long ago had that been. Was I the only one who ventured into the mountains? The only one who had chosen to take the right hand trail at the fork?

I shrugged, that didn't seem likely. I looked at my pack, and the mess it was in. I really should clean that out before I had to make the trip back home. I stretched out my back, the vertebrae popping, and walked over to the messy pack. I took out the hide and stretched it over the ground. I was so proud that I had gotten a gift from the spirits and couldn't wait to tell Grandpa and Grandma about it. I hoped they'd believe me.

I tipped over the pack, which when filled right could stretch as long as me, and I am 5-feet-2-inches. I tipped out everything that was inside. The contents spilled onto the hide on the ground. There wasn't all that much, as most of the stuff was just little odds and ends. The biggest things were my tent that folded up and my parka which left a lot of room when they weren't in the pack. I laid out my rations. I had four days to go, and we had eaten most of what Grandma and I had packed. I smothered a giggle because Grandma packed for two weeks and that was fourteen days. What could I say, Midnight sure did eat a lot. Something small wrapped in moosehide caught my eye. What was that? I didn't remember packing it. In a flash I recalled it was the gift given to me by the elder. I knelt and examined the nicely wrapped bundle. I opened it slowly and unfolded the wrap. Out rolled a beautiful riverbed stone, blood red as ruby.

When I touched the stone, a bright flash blinded me. The sky went black, dark with flashes of lighting and the thunder roared. The rain poured down hard, bouncing off the ground. I caught my breath, afraid to move or breathe. The woman was standing there once again, with her black mouth open. She pointed at me, and my heart pounded. I couldn't move, only watch. She continued to point at me, and an ugly, creepy deep voice emerged from her mouth.

"For The blood of the innocent that was shed. Only the blood of the wrong must be paid. Only then the sickness of the "wrong" can be healed."

The vision released me, and I snapped back to my campsite and reality, holding the stone that was now black in my hand. My head was light, white sparks dancing before my eyes and I fell backwards. I lay on the ground, heart beating like a drum, while I gasped for air. In the sky the clouds gathered. I realized that things were starting to come together, starting to make a little more sense. I rolled over and scrambled to grab my diary. I needed to write down everything I could remember while it was still fresh in my mind. I wrote out what she said, word for word, and tried to make sense of it all. No matter how many times I looked at her words, the answer to the mystery, or the secret, danced around me but I just couldn't get it to reveal itself.

Just then Midnight came out of the tent, stretched, yawned, and headed for the usual marking of his territory. I wrote it all out in my diary again, my thoughts and my somewhat confused conclusions. My heart was still beating faster than normal. What a vision! I put the diary down and look at the time: 5:15pm. I called Midnight, he came with his ears up.

"Hunt," I told him.

Tail in the air, he hit the trail running. I looked at the mess strewn around me. I better clean this up. I started packing up and placed everything into the pack nicely. I even made room for extra things for the journey home. I sat in the tent when I was finished and tried to make sense of all the dreams and visions. I got up and added more wood to the fire, then returned to the tent and took out my notes again. Somehow it was all connected, the women, a glimpse of her life, the blood and the riddle, the flowers, the herbs, my grandpa dying, elders dying, some of them gone crazy. It was a lot to take in. I kept reading, I almost had enough for a book.

I stared at the first dream I had, the falls with the blood in the water, I started thinking about the girl's life, how sad and lonely she must have been, all alone. My heart ached for her. I read about how she fell in love and how devastated she was when he turned his back on her. I tamped down a flare of anger and kept reading. She lost her mother at a very young age and only knew what she had been taught. Somehow, she managed to survive by herself in the woods without someone to care for her. Reading on, I came to a dream I had written out. It was the part where she lost her unborn baby and was bleeding out. My mind jumped to my last vision about the blood. Is that what she meant? The blood of the innocent? Did she mean her baby?

I started putting my thoughts down on a new page. I got so engrossed in my search for some clarity I lost track of time. It was 6pm and it had started to get dark. Where did the day go? Midnight came running back with a fresh rabbit in his mouth. It had taken him a bit of time to hunt this one down.

"Good boy." I patted him on the head, and he grinned at me.

I set the diary aside and got up. I threw more wood on the fire, took the rabbit from Midnight, and started dinner. After we ate. we headed out to get rid of the rabbit remains. I pushed through the bush, heading towards the back edge of the water. I had to bury the remains.well, and far away from the campsite. After piling some stones on the disturbed dirt, Midnight and I started back to our camp. We were on the trail by the falls when rocks started coming down. Midnight jumped and barked at the falls. I grabbed my gun and looked at top side of the falls. I swore I could see the shadow, or outline, of a woman. I blinked and looked again, now I couldn't see anyone, or anything, in the gathering dark. I shrugged. It must have just been loose rocks coming down as the colder night air replaced the heat of the day. Midnight had calmed down, so we carried on. It was late, and I was tired, By the time we got back to the tent, the stars were out, and the moon was rising. In the mountains at this time of year, the sun was gone by 6pm, and the stars and moon took over around 7pm. I threw more wood on the fire before I crawled into the tent with Midnight and called it a night.

Was I ever going to be able to sleep again without dreams or visions? The young girl was alone in the hut, after her mother had passed. Even in the dream I was aware of the timeline. She was boiling rabbit soup on the fire. She remembered her mother's words and was teaching herself how to survive.

A knock on the door drew her attention. Her friend entered and I recognized him as the boy she used to play with, though he was older now too. She cried and told him what happened to her mother. He offered comfort and promised her he would always check on her to make sure she was safe.

Fog rolled in and covered everything. The next thing I saw was the girl and the boy. They were older now and still seeing one another secretly. They met by the falls and made love. He promised her they would be together in a few moons. He said he loved her and didn't care what his father said.

The scene switched with a jump that startled me. A man yelled at the now young man who was his son, "You will never see that girl again. She is a witch, a windigo. I am pledging you to the medicine man's daughter to secure our future." The young man was angry but knew he must listen to his father.

Chapter Nine

Day Nine

The alarm woke me at 6:30am. I reached for my diary to get the dream written inside before it faded. When I finished, I lay back down and reset the alarm for 8:am. Sure as the sun, the alarm went off at 8:am. My mind was ready to face the day, but my body had other ideas. My limbs were weak as if I hadn't slept in days. My bones hurt and my back ached. I forced myself to move and rolled out of the tent. I stretched my back until every bone cracked.

Midnight did the same, shaking his head. "I know, right?" I grinned at him.

I decided I needed to find out why my dreams were being haunted by the strange woman. By this time I was getting to know some of her story from the dreams and visions. I was learning a side of the story that was never told in our village by the storyteller and elders. There was another story here--her story.

My stomach growled interrupting my thoughts. I looked at my dog. "Shall we go find some rabbits?"

He jumped up as if I said candy. I laughed, and he barked happily, leaping from side to side. I picked up my gun.

Midnight's antics said it all, he wanted to hunt. I set out with him, and he ran ahead. The dog was amazing at scenting prey. I walked the trail, gun in hand, ready for action. The sound Midnight was making let me know he was on the chase. I crouched down and listened. There was a lot of wrestling and crashing in the bush, about twenty feet from me. Midnight must have got something. I waited and a few minutes later he came out with a rabbit in his mouth. I didn't know how he did it, but that dog sure could hunt those rabbits. It was his favorite sport.

I smiled and petted his head. "Good Boy!"

He heard something in the bush, his ears perked up, he barked and ran off again through the trees. I waited again while I put the rabbit in the bag I brought. Twigs broke nearby, Midnight popped his head through the bush with another rabbit.

"I think that's good, boy."

I took the rabbit and stuffed it in the bag. He sat there giving me a huge doggy smile. I loved him so much. Midnight was truly my best friend.

We headed back to the campsite to start on the rabbits. I walked slowly and took close notice of my surroundings. My gaze fell on a patch of wild mushrooms, and I stooped to pick a few. To the right were some wild carrots. I'd been so busy I'd never even noticed them before. There were berries, herbs, green onions, thyme, rosemary, parsley, wild garlic, herbs of all sorts. Among them were flowers of purple, yellow, pink, and red, growing in between the roots. There were flowers that looked like shoes, stars, bells, and rose buds, the smell was fresh and beautiful. I couldn't believe all these plants grew here. Some of these plants were rare and hard to find. I had a herb book back at home in the village so I could find out what some of these were when I got back. I started picking, just a handful of each making sure not to strip the patch. It was about 10:am when I got back to the campsite and started cooking. I skinned and gutted the rabbits and chopped up everything. I made a meal to fill us both with plenty of leftovers for another meal later. We were both full, but we went off to bury the remains away from camp as we always did. The sun was noon high in the sky and it was a beautiful day. I debated on whether I should walk off the big meal or crawl into the tent for a nap. Nap almost won, but if I did that I would be up all night. I voted to go for a walk. I called Midnight, took the gun and tucked my diary in a pocket in case I needed to record anything important. I was curious about that trail and wanted to check it out for myself. I headed towards the dark side of the falls where I always seemed to see and hear weird stuff. I walked to the edge, pulled out my ribbons and tied one next to the ribbon I had put there earlier, just in case. I started down the trail, the undergrowth and trees had a dark, musty damp feeling, as if I were being covered with the earth's blanket. I kept moving forward, stepping over roots that were bigger than my legs. I kept calm and took every step with caution. Midnight padded along behind me. A crow called somewhere in the trees. I kept moving through the dark part of the trail and came a small clearing closer to the mountain. Just like in my dream I discovered a grave site. It was covered in thick rope like vines that grew all over the ground. The hairs rose on the back of my neck, but I kept my cool. There must be answers around here somewhere. I examined everything closely without disturbing anything, then walked past softly. I made my way to a mountain side trail that led onward. I followed it, but Midnight didn't like it at all, he trailed behind me whining his displeasure. I stayed on the trail as it led me higher into the mountain. It turned to the side where a narrow path brought me to a cave opening. My heart kicked in my chest and Midnight barked a warning. "Stay," I told him. He whined but did what I said.

I scrambled up the steep path with Midnight still barking behind me. I ignored him and kept going. By the time I reached the cave mouth I was breathing hard and my muscles protested. I took a deep breath to slow my breathing, kept my gun ready and paused in the dark opening. The opening led into a huge open cave, with a fire pit. It could be quite cozy if it was fixed up. There was a big round room with an opening right through the top where you could see the sky and smoke could escape from the fire. The only way out was the way I came in. The cave looked as it has been lived in years ago, before my time. I sat down for a second waiting to see if anything spoke to me. Other than the cool temperature of the cave, all was quiet. Midnight was still barking but stayed where I left him. I stood up and offered a silent farewell. I rejoined Midnight, who quit barking as soon as he saw me. We headed back down the mountain. I didn't stop at the grave site, just went right back to my camp. It was 4:30pm by the time we got back, and the light was fading. I started the fire and heated up the leftovers. After we ate, I laid in the tent with Midnight and recorded what I had discovered and where I had found it. I did some more reading and around 8:pm I crawled into my sleeping bag and went to sleep.

* * *

Again, somehow I knew it was a dream, even though it seemed so real. I recognized the man as my great grandfather from the photos Grandpa had at home. The man looked a lot like my grandpa. He was wrapping a stone knife he had made as a gift for someone special. I watched him walk down the trail toward the hut I always saw in these dreams. He looked around as if to be sure no one was watching before he knocked on the hut door. The door opened and he rushed in. A girl giggled as he closed the door. Unnoticed, I followed him inside, slipping through the door. Inside, he presented the girl with his gift. Her happiness was evident as she hugged him. They gazed into each other's eyes, then grabbed on to each other, kissing wildly, and ripping each other's clothes off. The way they embraced and made passionate love to each other made me blush, but I had to keep watching. I knew what was about to happen was important. Afterward, they lay quiet and held each other close. She told him she was with child, as she lay a hand on her belly. Shock and displeasure flared across his features, and he sat up fast.

"Are you sure?" he demanded.

"Yes, I'm sure. I missed one full moon of bleeding. Are you not happy about the news?" The happiness in her face was replaced with confusion.

"Yes, I am happy, but my father will banish me if he knows of this. He has already chosen the medicine man's daughter to be my bride. That was why I came to you tonight, to say goodbye."

Panic and outrage radiated from her. "What do you mean? You said we would be together after six moons, and I believed you. I am carrying your child, what am I to do now?" She took a ragged breath. "The elders will banish me, or worse yet, kill me and my unborn," her voice broke in sorrow and fear,

"I don't know...I don't know what to do now." He scrambled to his feet, pulling his clothes on as he did.

"I can't come back. I can't see you anymore. Why weren't you more careful? You knew what herbs to use..."

The girl got to her feet and grabbed his arm, pleading with him to stay with her and their baby. Sobs tore at her chest. The man, my great grandfather, ripped her hand from him and knocked her to the floor.

"No! Stay away from me, now and forever." He stormed out of the hut, leaving the door gaping open behind him.

The girl lay where she fell, weeping. Finally, she gathered her clothes and dressed. Picking up the stone knife, she threw it outside and slammed the door. She slid down the door to collapse on the floor. I could hear her whispering to herself. "What am I going to do now? I'm in so much trouble and I'm scared." Something changed in the quality of the dream, it was as if she suddenly realized I was there. Anger contorted her features, and she surged to her feet, eyes black as a starless night. The girl picked up a cup and unerringly threw it straight at my head.

Chapter Ten

Day Ten

My own scream woke me up, Midnight cowering beside me. I stroked his head in apology and reached for my diary. I needed to write every little detail down before I forgot anything that might be important. I checked my watch and was astounded to see it was eight in the morning. I peeked outside the tent to see the sun and confirm the time. It was indeed morning. After I recorded everything I could remember I closed my tired eyes and rested until noon.

I blinked and opened my eyes. My shirt was wet with sweat, so I sat up and unzipped my parka. A glance at my watch told me it was 12pm. Judging by the state of my clothes, it must be hot today. I unzipped the tent, and Midnight flew out of the opening. That dog must have to go do his business really bad.

I lay on my back and sighed. Two more days, that was all I had left. If I didn't get any answers, what would I tell my elders? My Grandpa, who was so sick? The dark specter of failure threatened to overwhelm me, but I gritted my teeth. "

"No, I can't give up," I said sternly. I got up and crawled out of the tent. I pulled my pack out, along with my sleeping bag and my parka. I hung them over some branches to air them out before I started the fire.

I had to figure this out. There was no other option. I made myself a coffee and rolled a smoke. It had been days since I set out and I needed to think. Midnight was back, and he sat looking at me.

"Hunt!" He trotted off, hopefully to do what I told him. I watched the fire and sipped on my coffee trying to wake up. I took a few more drags of my smoke, and suddenly, pieces started to fall into place.

I jumped to my feet, heart racing with excitement. "I got it! I know it. That's what it's got to be. How did I not see this before?"

I grabbed my book, pen, and map. Sitting back down I ripped out all my notes and started to sort them out like a puzzle. I laid them all down on the ground, and one by one started reading them in order. My breath caught in my chest and my vision wavered for a moment. The shock forced me to put my head down in my hands. The man in the visions and dreams...he was my great, great, grandfather. And the girl in the woods, she was the witch.

I let myself fall into the vision.

My eyes turned white, and I could see it all from front to back. Who was in the wrong and who the woman was, what she experienced. I saw it all, the pain, the heartbreak, the loss of her child, and her mother. My grandfather walking away from her, abandoning her. Through her eyes, from where she hid in the tree line by the village, I watched him wed another woman. Everything was so clear, and I realized what I needed to do. Tears for her wet my cheeks, and the woman, the witch, stepped into my vision, clearer than the memories, and pointed to the falls of blood.

I shook myself free of the vision, tears still damp on my face. I looked around my campsite and realized I was in the spot where it all happened. It was my duty to help her move on from the pain my great-great-grandfather caused her. Here, marked on this beautiful part of our land, it was clear to me what I must do. I gathered up my knife and sage, along with the stone that was given to me, and headed to the falls.

Once I got to the edge of the falls, I lit the sage and said a prayer of protection before smudging myself well. I walked into the pool at the base of the falls and sat in the water. I let her sorrow creep over me. Soaking into my emotions. I lifted my hand with the knife clasped in my other hand. I closed my free hand over the blade and pulled hard and fast. The pain was swift, hot and cold, at the same time, then the blood came staining the water around me red. The woman appeared in front of me. I looked up at her.

"I feel your pain, and I am sorry for what my great-great-grandfather, and the others, did to you. I hope I can make it right by offering my own blood in apology to ask for your forgiveness." I spoke, surprised my voice was so steady.

I held my hand up, blood running freely down my wrist and forearm. As every drop hit the water, the witch cried, head bowed. Then she looked up at me and the sky cleared. The sun shone on her, and she was no longer ugly and old, but beautiful with glowing black hair as long as the river.

She smiled at me. "Thank you," she whispered and walked away.

I felt free, at peace, and I could think clearly. I raised my eyes to the top of the falls. The elder who gave me the gift in my earlier vision was standing there. He smiled, waved farewell, and disappeared into the trees. It was done. I was sure the witch had accepted my apology and the sacrifice of my blood. The taste of her forgiveness was tangible in the misty air.

I threw the stone from the elder back into the falls. I needed to rest now, my journey was hard, and I lost a lot of blood. I stumbled back to the tent and pulled out the box of supplies. I bandaged my hand and sang a song of healing in my tongue. I was proud of myself, but I didn't get any answers about the healing stuff for my grandpa. "Please let him be okay. How does this work? Did I do all this journeying and somehow he was just all better?" Were there plants I should pick? Suddenly, I was lost again, after all that. I shook my head in disappointment.

Midnight trotted back into camp with his rabbit. I laughed. "You're going to be so fat on rabbits if I keep you here much longer."

He barked as if he was answering me. I started talking to him as if he was a person, telling him everything I had just been through. I needed to talk to someone. He kept his eyes on me the whole time I talked, as if he was listening to my every word. I stopped and hugged him, kissed him all over, and gave him a big piece of Bannock for a snack till I cooked his rabbit. I love my dog so much.

I looked at the time, it was only 2pm. Wow, how could I be so tired now? I just got up at noon, the experience at the falls must have taken more out of me than I thought.

I decided to cook that rabbit. So, I prepared it, started the fire, and just when I was about to wrap up the remains, out of the tree line stepped a huge bear. It stood straight up and looked at me, sniffing the air. Midnight jumped and barked at it. I carefully edged towards the tent, and slowly bent down. Midnight kept his attention on the bear. I grabbed my gun, my heart beating like crazy, I lifted the gun, stood up, and took the safety off. I pointed the gun at the bear. "Get out of here," I yelled as loud as I could.

The bear sniffed the air and let out a roar at Midnight. I whistled for my dog and

Midnight came to me, backing away, his gaze never leaving the bear.

"Stop barking," I hissed at him, but he continued to bark.

That just got the bear more annoyed. I fired two rounds in the air, my ears rang, and the sound echoed through the mountains. Thank goodness it scared the bear, and he turned and ran back into the bush. I'm not sure what I would have done if he hadn't left.

I took a deep breath and let out a sigh of relief. That was too close. Foolishly, I had let my guard down and it almost cost me. My hands were still shaking. I finished wrapping up the remains, then Midnight and I headed out to bury it--further from camp this time. Once we got back to the campsite, I cooked up the rabbit but stayed on guard. I fed the fire and cleaned my site before I started packing, ready for my travel back home tomorrow.

I had to leave tomorrow afternoon if I wanted to make the next camp site. It was a day to get there and another day to get home. If I didn't show up on time, my grandpa and uncle were to meet me or come find me. I didn't want them to worry about me.

I looked at the time it was 3:30. I had a lot of room in my pack and wanted to bring home some rabbits for Grandma. I decided we should get some on our way home tomorrow. I smiled and sat there for a moment savoring the comfort of the place. I didn't want to leave but I had my map now. I knew where to find this place again. I would be back and bring my uncle. I went to the falls and filled my water container with fresh water, Midnight filling up by my side. I laughed at him. We strolled back to the campsite. I found some high bush berries and picked a few. I realized there was tons everywhere, so I took a small bag out my pack and started picking. Within no time I had gathered a bag full. My grandma loved these berries, and she only got some once in a while when my uncle brought them home. She would be so pleased with my gift. Proudly, I tucked them in the pack, then decided I better get dinner. Midnight and I went to the far side of the water, where the water from the falls gathered in a lake. Good fishing here, I thought. I threw out the fishing line and three casts later I hooked a fish. I pulled that line in fast; the fish was a nice one.

I gave Midnight a happy look. "Now it's my turn to provide dinner." I laughed at him as he jumped around. We walked back and I hadn't realized how far back around the falls we had gone. Good thing we were by the water and could follow it back, or I'd be lost.

I should know better, I thought to myself. We walked back to our camp and Midnight jumped into the tent. I shook my head at him and smiled. I built up the fire until it was going good. I started to clean the fish and pulled the tin foil out of my pack in the tent. I wrapped the fish well and put in the ring of stones by the side of the hot fire with two stones to hold it up. We ate when it was done, the sun was going down. I checked the time: 5:45pm. I took out my diary and recorded the events of the day, as Midnight slept by my side. The fire was warm, and the moon made its way into the sky, peeking through the branches of the trees before it broke free into the sable sky. It was so peaceful. I packed up my gear ready for my journey home tomorrow.

I called it a night, banked the fire, and crawled into my sleeping bag in the tent. I pulled out my book and did some reading. By 7pm I was getting sleepy, and I was ready for home. I fell into a deep sleep.

Once again, I knew I was dreaming, but somehow it was more than just a dream. It was the same dream I had before. The old lady was in the forest with the little girl, but this time she was looking right at me and invited me to watch. She knew I was there and accepted me. She was teaching us both about the herbs and the flowers growing in the mountains. She spoke to us both.

"These flowers only grow for a few years before they have to rest and renew themselves. They are only found here in these mountains. If mixed and blended right, you can heal the sick of all kinds of ailments." She pointed at the purple flowers and the white star like flowers. "Go ahead and pick as much as you can carry," she encouraged us. "But first," she said, "We mix. I will show you." The woman brought out a bowl, put some of both of the flowers in it, and crushed them finely with a stone. Then she added water from the falls, then the thyme, before she crushed them into a paste. She looked at me and said, "You must boil it and set it aside until it cools, then have the person drink it. The sick person will sleep for a day, but they will heal."

I smiled at her, she smiled back and said, "Now you must go, my child. Our paths have come to an end." She walked away through the forest with the little girl at her side. The girl looked back and waved at me. "Bye."

I waved back and woke up. I had the answer now, I knew what to look for, and what to do with it when I found it. I rolled over and went back to sleep.

Chapter Eleven

Day 11

I woke up early, and I knew exactly where to go. I almost vibrated with excitement and relief. I knew where to find what I was looking for. And most importantly, I knew how to mix it. I could heal my grandpa! Wow, I thought. I could be a healer if I really tried, there were things and plants here in these mountains that no one knew about. I could learn them all. I jumped with excitement. I looked at the time: 8am.

I had time after breakfast to go picking what I needed. I looked at Midnight. "Want to go get our breakfast?" He barked in reply. I opened the tent and said, "Hunt!" He took off, tail waving happily.

I got out of the tent and looked around. Taking a deep breath, I stretched, and let my mind go back to the dream. Excitement coursed through me. I knew where the flowers were and couldn't wait to get a bit more sunlight through the forest trees before I went searching. I shook out my sleeping bag, rolled it up along with the parka, and the tent. Everything fit in my pack and there was still lots of room. It was 9:10am; Midnight should have been back by now. Hands on my hips, I whistled loudly, after a few minutes he came running. Yup, he got his rabbit. I laughed at him, gave him a hug, and rubbed his back and head.

"Good boy!"

I cooked up the rabbit and we ate sitting side by side at the fire. It was a good meal for our last one in this place. I thanked Midnight and asked him if he was ready. He gave me a huge doggy smile. I laughed at him.

"We're going to pick the flowers and herbs now," I told him.

I grabbed a bigger bag that was tucked in the pack and picked up my gun. Together, we headed out, down the trail where we hunted last time. That was where I had found all the carrots and garlic and herbs. We kept walking through the forest, and I started harvesting the items I needed as we came to them. I picked so much of each item that my bag was heavy with plants and herbs.

I was pleased with my morning. Midnight and I headed back to camp. Once there, I packed up the plants and herbs carefully so they would be safe in my pack. I stopped and took one more look around. A sigh escaped my lips. "I'll be back," I promised. I hefted my pack on my back, gun in my hand, Midnight by my side, we headed down the trail following the bright orange ribbons leading my way.

It took a good day of walking, during which we stopped a few times to rest as the pack was heavy. I didn't mind though, I kept going, taking water and snack breaks. The sun was starting to lower into the top of the tree line. A look at my watch told me it was 4:30pm. I consulted my map. I still had at least an hour to go before reaching our destination. I put the map away and we kept going, following the markers, moving along as fast as I could manage.

I made it to the campsite I was aiming for just in time to make a fire before the light failed. I popped up the tent and pulled out the parka. Walking down the mountain it seemed to get colder, which was odd. It should be colder up at the higher elevation, then down here. I shrugged it off and looked at the time again: 6:35pm. I pulled out the pack and dug out some Bannock and dried meat. The supplies were running low. Midnight and I ate and tucked in for the night, we were so tired, we went right to sleep.

Chapter Twelve

Day 12
The alarm woke me at 8:am. I opened my eyes, blinked and stretched. I felt great, rested and ready to tackle the long hike ahead of me today.

Midnight was still lying beside me. I rolled over and gave him a hug.

"Come on boy, we've got another full day of hiking to do."

I wriggled out of my sleeping bag and unzipped the tent. The morning air was cold with the breath of spring. I shivered and started the fire. Once I had it going nice and big and hot I stood for a moment just listening.

Shaking my head, I decided to start on some coffee. I was 7 hours away from home and Uncle and Grandpa should be heading this way by now. Today would be a good day to hunt as I wanted to bring some meat home for Grandma. I grinned at Midnight and said the word he loved so much.

"Hunt!"

He took off like a shot. Smiling I got to work cleaning up my site and packing up. I leaned my pack against the wood pile, checked my gun, and started to explore around the area where we'd camped last night. I had my ribbons to help get me back if I got turned around. I set out in the opposite direction that Midnight ran off in, just in case he chased something out.

I kept low and quiet, watched my step, and listened. Through the trees I could hear Midnight on the chase. I let him be, he knew if I wasn't at the site he would drop the rabbit and wait or go out to find more. After all it was a hunting day. There was some rustling in the bushes, I looked deep and slowly crept over. A partridge was foraging under a berry bush. I took aim and shot. Perfect hit. I went over and picked it up, keeping my eye out in case there was more. Not likely as anything else that was around would have scattered at the sound of the gunshot.

I made my way back to the camp. Sure enough Midnight had left his kill there. I put the rabbit and chicken in the pack. I sat for a minute and listened. Midnight came dashing up with another rabbit. What a dog! I laughed at him, took the rabbit and packed it with the rest. My stomach growled, reminding me I hadn't eaten yet. Midnight flopped down beside me, he looked like he wanted a nap. I gave him some water and then looked at the time: 11am.

"Well buddy, let's get you something to eat and hunt a bit more."

I dug some food out of the pack to snack on.

When we'd finished eating we set out on the hunt again. Midnight had all the luck, getting 8 rabbits that morning. I only managed 2 chickens. I giggled, some hunter I was, my dog did better than me.

I checked the time: 1:pm. I cocked my head at Midnight. "Shall we head to the next site and call it a day?"

He barked in agreement, and we headed down the trail. About two hours later I met up with my uncle on the trail, he was alone.

"Where's Grandpa?" I said. Worry clenching my guts.

Uncle met my gaze and shook his head. "He's not doing well, but it's going to be okay. Why don't you tell me about your journey so far."

I tried to keep my worry and fear from showing on my face, so I smiled, and together we headed down a hill. Before long we arrived at the campsite Uncle had already set up.

I thought we'd just camp here for the night," Uncle said.

I was happy he was there with me. We set up my tent and Uncle built the fire and started the coffee. It was nice having someone else make the fire and coffee. I laughed, happy with the companionship.

Uncle looked from the fire. "What's so funny?"

"It's just nice to have another person around after twelve days," I told him.

Uncle grinned. "You get used to being alone," he said.

After the fire was ready, I pulled out a rabbit. Uncle laughed at me.

"Awe, how cute," he joked, like I was pulling a rabbit out of a hat.

I laughed too. "At least I made it this long alone," I said.

Midnight barked and I had to give him his due. "Okay, well maybe not alone."

Uncle pulled out a pouch of tobacco. "You still have some?" he asked.

"A bit, I hardly smoked out here," I replied.

He smiled. "That's good." Uncle rolled a couple of smokes and gave me one. We lit up and sat together, watching the flames leap in the fire. It was nice to relax and enjoy his silent company while we sipped coffee and smoked.

Giving me a sideways glance, Uncle grinned. "Are you going to cook that rabbit or just eat it raw?"

I laughed, finished my coffee and smoke and started prepping it. In no time I had cooked a nice meal and Uncle was happy and full. I cleaned up while Uncle got rid of the rabbit remains. When I was finished, Midnight and I sat by the fire. When Uncle came back he had a small bag of spruce gum for Grandpa.

"Well, looks like I'm not the only one looking for medicine out here," I said.

He joined us by the fire, threw more wood on, and asked me to tell him the story of my journey. I reached in my pack and pulled out my diary.

"What is that?" Uncle had a funny look on his face.

"I kept notes on everything that happened, just like a book," I told him.

He smiled and rolled another smoke. "Okay, tell me."

I sat across from him with my diary and started reading my dreams and visions while he sat and listened for hours. We talked about many things, his journey as a boy with his dad in these mountains, and he told tales of things I had yet to see. As time went by, the sun went down.

Uncle yawned and stretched. "It's time to call it a night. Thank you for sharing your stories with me." He crawled in his tent.

Midnight, and I crawled into ours. The night was so peaceful, I could hear the owls, their voices lulled me into sleep.

Chapter Thirteen

Day 13

I got up at 8am. Uncle had already packed his tent and was ready to head out.

"Are you going to wait for me?" I joked.

He laughed. "Of course, you have the rabbits."

I grinned and started rolling up my things and organizing the pack.

"You must eat before we go," Uncle said.

By the fire, he already had a rabbit cooked and coffee ready for me. *Man, what time did he get up?* I thanked him and ate everything he had prepared. Then I finished packing and we headed out toward home. Uncle led the way, with Midnight behind me. We were making good time. I checked my watch: 11:am. Uncle stopped and raised his hand in the air. I stopped too and listened.

"We need to rest a minute." Uncle threw his pack down and sat on it. He pulled out his pouch and started rolling a smoke. I threw my pack down beside him and laid on it. "Oh my God, my back," I groaned.

"So, what do you have in that pack that makes it so heavy?" Uncle asked.

I looked at him and smiled. "A lot!"

Uncle looked down the trail, and then at the position of the sun in the sky. "We should be home by five or six."

I took a drink of water and gave some to Midnight. Uncle took the lead again, I walked behind him, with Midnight behind me, so we stayed close together on the trail. We'd been walking a while when I looked at the time: 2:pm.

"Uncle, I need to stop for a minute," I called.

He looked at the sun and nodded. "Okay, we can rest for twenty minutes."

My back was on fire from the weight of the pack, my stomach growling with hunger. I collapsed on the ground, rolled over and dug in the pack until I found the last bag of dried meat, and one piece of bannock. I shoved the food in my mouth, so hungry I forgot to give Midnight a snack too. Uncle pulled a big bag of food out of his pack. I was so happy to see that. He passed the bag over and I took another bannock for me and gave Midnight his. I felt better now my stomach was full. Uncle checked the position of the sun again. "We have only a few more hours till the sun is down."

"Okay." I sighed and lifted my pack. We continued along the trail, while we walked the sun slowly went down. It was almost five, but we were close to home now. I could see my grampa's trail. Not much further to go. I managed to keep up with my uncle as he increased his pace. We were getting close to the village now. I could hear the dogs barking and smell wood smoke. We couldn't be more than fifteen minutes out. Excitement gave me a burst of energy.

I just wanted to run home to Grandma. Finally, I could see our house. We made it! Tonight, I would sleep in my bed with warm blankets and a pillow. It was 5:30, we made it, just as uncle said we would. As we got closer to the house, I could see that the lights were on, smoke was coming out of the chimney. Midnight pranced with excitement. When we got closer to the house, Uncle told me to tie Midnight up. I took him over to his doghouse in the back. He gave a sad look.

"I know boy, but we're home," I said. I petted him, gave him a hug, and went inside. I walked through the door and the smell of fried moose meat was in the air. I inhaled deeply, my mouth watering. I put my pack down and went to my grandma's room. She was sitting on the bed beside Grandpa who was under the covers. I bent down and gave her a hug. I lay on the bed, reached for my grandpa, and gave him a kiss.

He smiled. You have to tell me all about it when I'm feeling better."

"I will," I promised.

Grandma took my hand and led me out, she looked worried.

"I have some things for you," I said.

Her face lit up with joy when I dug out the berries, the huge bag of herbs and flowers, and all the rabbits and chickens. Uncle put the rabbits and chickens away in the back porch.

Grandma was so pleased with the berries. She took a plate out of the cupboard and fed me at the table. Moose meat and fried bannock. Then she fussed over me. She took my dirty socks off and gave me clean clothes to put on and brought me hot tea to help warm me up. I loved my grandma so much. She was my mom. It was Grandma who raised me after my mom ran off with a man when I was a child.

"When did Grandpa get so sick?" I asked.

"Four days after you left," she told me.

Oh my God! That was when I started having those dreams and visions. I looked at the time, it was 6:45 going on to 7:pm. I told Grandma about the dream and the instructions about the medicine and how to prepare it. I asked her to help me. We followed the directions I'd written down; powdered up the ingredients and boiled the water. I mixed it all up in a cup and told Grandma to get Grandpa to drink it all.

She nodded and brought it to him. Grandma propped Grandpa up with pillows while he sipped it and she made sure he drank it all down. He fell asleep right away.

"Is he okay? Is that right?" Grandma asked, worry creasing her face.

"Yes, it's the medicine. It will take a day to work and he will sleep through it"

"Better not poison him," Uncle said cheekily when he came in. He helped himself to some tea.

Grandma looked tired. I didn't think she was feeling well herself.

"Do you need anything?" I asked.

"Rest! Could you clean up the kitchen for me before you go to bed?"

"Of course," I said."

Grandma went to her room and closed the door.

Uncle got up. "Time for bed." He went to his room, closing the door behind him.

It was up to me then. I cleaned the kitchen and then hung the herbs to dry in the back. I finished up, went to my room, and got undressed. It was nice to be so warm I thought as I put on my night gown and crawled into my bed. Oh my God, the feeling of clean sheets and a mattress and pillow was amazing after 12 days on the ground.

I stretched my legs between the sheets and the comforter felt like clouds. I giggled, turned over and fell asleep.

Chapter Fourteen

Day 14

I slept so well and felt amazing the next morning. I could smell bacon and fresh coffee and toast. Grandma was up.

I yawned and lingered for a moment more, it was so nice to be back in a bed and not sleeping on the ground. I got up and got dressed. I couldn't wait to start the day and tell my story. I wanted to see my cousins and tell them all about my journey. I put on my slippers and went out to the kitchen. Grandma was at the stove. Grandpa was still sleeping. I checked in on him, he was sleeping peacefully. I checked the time: 8:30am. Maybe he would sleep till afternoon, or later?

Uncle came in from outside. "Good morning, sleep well?"

"Yes, I did."

"I know, I could hear you snoring from my room." He grinned.

Heat rose in my face, and I smiled. "Cheeky!"

Grandma smiled at me. "What did you do with everything you brought back?"

I showed her where I put it all, she nodded, pleased that I put it all away correctly.

She set a plate of breakfast in front of me. "Eat."

It was nice to be home, I ate everything. It felt like I hadn't eaten in days.

Grandma smiled. "You were hungry!"

"I was, all I've eaten lately is rabbits and dried meat."

'That's how we used to eat when we lived in the mountains. Come sit by me, have a coffee, and tell me about your journey, I want to hear your story."

I was so proud; I was the first in the history of our family to undertake a journey this young, alone, and a woman yet. My grandma was so eager to hear my story. I grabbed a coffee, went to my room and took out my diary. Just when I got back to the kitchen someone knocked on the door. Grandma opened it, it was my two cousins, Jimmy and Ashton, coming to see me.

Grandma let them in. "You're just in time for your cousin's story. Come in and have something to drink."

My cousin Ashton was one year behind me, and soon he, and Jimmy too, would go on their own journey and have their own stories to tell. We gathered on my grandparent's couch by the wood stove and Grandma sipped her coffee. My cousins took a spot on the floor. I sat by my grandma with my legs crossed, took a sip of my coffee, then

I started with the first night recorded in my diary.

Grandma sat there with a wide smile as I read on through the pages. She gasped when I came to the dream of the old woman by the falls.

I looked over at Grandma. "What?"

"A few months ago, your grandpa started having dreams, and that was when he started getting sick. He spoke of this dream too. A group of women by a waterfall." Grandma's voice was hushed and almost cautious.

My cousins sat on the floor looking at us with their mouths wide open.

"There is a boy in the village that has been seeing an old woman in his dreams, and his dad is sick too now," Jimmy said.

My grandma got up. "I think you should go now and come back later. Grandpa will be getting up soon," she told my cousins.

"But the story was just getting good," Ashton whined.

Grandma looked distressed, so I stepped in for her. "I'll continue the story later. Don't worry, I'll tell you everything."

My cousins got up and hugged me and Grandma. "We missed you, we're happy you're back. Thank you for the tea, Grandma." Then they left.

A glance at the clock told me it was almost 10:am. Grandma went to check on Grandpa, he was still sleeping, but his color was coming back to his face. Grandma sighed with relief and touched his hand before she came out of the bedroom and closed the door. We sat at the table, and she put her hand in mine and gave me a soft look.

"I must hear more of this dream."

I got my diary from where I left it lying on the couch and then I rejoined her at the table.

"I am so happy the school has taught you how to read and write and be able to keep everything on paper. Good idea keeping that diary with you and writing things down so you would remember everything."

"Thank you for making sure I went to school. Now I can share what I learned with others." I smiled and opened the diary.

Wow, I had half a diary full just from that trip. I told Grandma everything from start to finish. After I came to the end, she sat quietly for a few minutes, thinking about what I said.

She cleared her throat and looked up at me. "I am proud and envious. I have been on my own journeys as a young woman, and never did I see or experience what you have. I had adventures with your grandfather when we were young, trying to find our own way as husband and wife, and working to start a family. My children have grown and left these lands, just your uncle stayed to help his dad. Not even my children have been as deep in those mountains, and yet you journey there and have spiritual visions. You have the gift of the healer in you to make such a journey."

I couldn't find the words to express how much her words moved me. They made me proud and gave me courage. I smiled at Grandma.

"Tell me more about the herbs," she asked me.

I told her everything the women taught me and her daughter in my dream. Grandma walked over to the herbs hanging to dry.

"I want to learn as much as I can about these and other herbs. There is a medicine man in our village. You should go pay him a visit," she said, looking over her shoulder at me.

Armed with the newfound courage her words had given me, I agreed. I got up and was surprised to see it was 12:20pm. We spent the whole morning talking. I felt so much closer to my grandma. A cough coming from Grandpa's room alerted us that he was waking up. Grandma was there by his side in seconds. He was awake and she handed him a cup of fresh hot coffee. He sat and his eyes looked clearer than they had for a while. He was obviously feeling so much better.

"Godiah," he called for me.

I went to him, and he opened his arms. I rushed in for the hug and held him close to me. He put his hands on both sides of my face.

"Thank you," he whispered. He sat back. "Sit, both of you, you must hear what I have dreamed."

I let out a gasp when he started, because I recognized the place he was describing. How could that be?

"It was by a huge waterfall in the forest. There was an old man there who greeted me and showed me a young girl making her journey. This girl had broken the curse bound to our family's bloodline. He showed me the woman who many called a witch, and her story was told to me in visions. My father's father was her love, my heart ached as I watched the pain of her loss. I saw that my granddaughter walked with her in a field of medicine that can heal our people" He looked at me with a tear rolling down his face. "I saw you, my little sprout." Pride radiated from his smile, he pulled my head down and kissed me on my forehead.

A lump formed in my throat and a soft sob escaped my lips. "Thank you, Grandpa."

"Thank you for saving this family," he said. Then he went on to relate about how sick his grandfather had gotten shortly after going crazy because of a women haunting his dreams. He died a few weeks after that, then the same thing happened to his father. When Grandpa was a boy, he watched his father go mad with the dreams and then the sickness that followed. He died a few weeks after the dreams started.

"I thought it was my time to go the same way," Grandpa said. He looked down and a few tears ran down his wrinkled cheeks. "I started having dreams a few months ago, and after you left to go to the mountains, they became horrible, and I did not understand them till now."

I grabbed hold of my grandpa and cried, both with grief and relief. I couldn't imagine our lives without him.

"It's all good now, I feel better and stronger, it is as if twenty years have been lifted from my shoulders."

I released him and smiled. Grandma hugged me.

"I knew you were special when you were born." She smiled. "Now, let's make something to eat."

We went to the kitchen, leaving Grandpa propped up on the couch now that he's feeling better. Grandma pulled out a big bowl along with the flour, baking powder, lard, and salt, I knew just by looking what she was making, her famous Bannock which I loved so much.

She went to the porch and brought in the four rabbits. Midnight's hunt. I looked out the window to see Midnight laying in the sun, head on his paws.

Awe my dog, I thought. I put together a huge bowl of mush for him. Grandma looked at me.

"I hope you're not feeding all that to just one dog."

I laughed. "Yes! Yes, I am, and you know why? Because that dog saved me in more ways than one, and he's a great hunter that needs his meals too.

My grandpa laughed hard from the couch drinking his coffee.

"He's her hunter." He winked at Grandma.

They both laughed at me. I took the food out to Midnight. He was so happy to see me and the food. When I set the bowl down he dug in hard. I petted my dog and gave him big rubs on his side as he ate.

* * *

Across the road was where my grandpa's friend lived. He was ill too, and his grandson, who was my age, was having the same dreams. Word had spread through the village of my return from the mountains. I was outside fixing the wood pile when an elder came walking down the road. It was the medicine man my grandma had spoken of., He saw me and came over.

"How is your grandpa doing?"

"He's fine," I said.

The elder looked at me a bit strange, and then walked over to the house across the road. He was doing a medicine trip for my grandpa's friend. I left the wood pile, walked over to Midnight and picked up his bowl. I hugged him and headed back inside. A few moments later there was a knock on the door. It was just 4:00pm. Grandpa asked Grandma to open the door and see who it was., When she opened the door, Joe, the medicine man, was standing there. Grandma invited him in. He greeted my grandpa and asked how he was. Grandpa told the medicine man that he felt younger and healthier than he had in a long time. Joe looked confused but then took the credit for my grandpa's well being.

Grandpa cleared his throat and sat up. "No disrespect my friend, but I was almost gone. My granddaughter made the journey to the mountain to pick the medicine herself for me. She brewed the tea for me, and I slept all day and woke up better."

The medicine man didn't look very impressed. He stared at me for a long moment, and it made me uncomfortable.

"You must come and talk with me. I would love to hear your story." He got up and said farewell to my grandpa and grandma. "I'll be seeing you later I hope," he said to me as he left the house. I could tell he was a bit resentful of me because Grandpa said I cured him and not Joe, but I shrugged it off.

"I think Joe might be worried about our little sprout being a medicine woman," Grandpa joked to Grandma and they both laughed.

I giggled because I hardly ever heard those two make jokes. Grandma was done with her bannock dough and was ready to put it in the oven.

"Help me with the rabbits," she asked.

"Okay, I'm pretty good at skinning them by now." I grinned.

She started on the potatoes and veggies, while I cut up the rabbits. We had just started dinner when Grandpa started asking me to tell him about my journey after dinner. That was the best time for storytelling, and I was happy he asked me to do story telling tonight. Usually, it was always him and Grandma telling the stories.

It was almost 5:pm when someone knocked on the door real hard. My cousin jimmy burst into the house, as if he was being chased.

"You okay?" Grandma asked him, getting up.

He gasped and caught his breath. "The old man wants you." He pointed at me.

"What old man?" I was confused.

"The medicine man, Joe, needs your help," Grandpa yelled.

"Me? What?" I still couldn't imagine what the medicine man thought I could do that he couldn't.

My grandma shooed me with her hands. "Hurry then, when Joe calls for help, you go."

I scrambled to get my shoes and jacket on and followed Jimmy to the house across the road. There were a lot of people gathered outside. I rushed past them with Grandma and Grandpa behind me. We no sooner got inside when the medicine man waved at me.

"Get over here. Move out of her way, I need her," he yelled.

Fear made my mouth dry, and I swallowed hard. What was going on?" Grandma wrapped an arm around me and Grandpa stood by my side. I looked down at the figure on the bed. It was Nambaa the boy from the village! He was having a vision of some sort; his eyes were open but white as snow with no iris showing. The medicine man knelt by his side. Joe appeared to be drained of energy, sweat soaking his shirt, he held out his hand.

"Clear the room," he ordered. "I need answers."

Everyone left but me, my grandparents, and Nambaa's parents.

"Has your journey to the mountain helped you and your family?" Joe asked me.

"Yes. Look at my grandpa," I replied.

"How is the woman in the dreams and visions tied to us all? And if you know what is happening now, you must speak," he told me.

Shock stole my breath; and I tried to speak. "I-I-I..."

"You must help us," Joe screeched as he and Nambaa fell to the floor.

I screamed, Grandpa held me up when my knees buckled. Nambaa's parents rushed to his side in tears, fear contorting their faces. The medicine man was on the floor out cold.

Oh my God!! What was going on? Terror sent my heart pounding, vibrating in my chest like a drum.

Then, the boy and Joe woke up. Questions I couldn't begin to answer came flying from everyone. I hid behind my grandpa.

"Slow down, you're scaring my granddaughter," Grandpa yelled.

That seemed to calm people down. Joe's wife brought tea to everyone. I noticed it was 7:40 in the evening. My stomach growled. We never did get a chance to eat dinner. I cleared my throat.

"What happened?

The medicine man, Joe replied, "This dream woman has been haunting our village and took most of our village a generation ago in sickness and madness, even death. She has come back once again to haunt us with things that we don't understand. Not even I understand what it is she wants." He lowered his head to hide his embarrassment.

"Can I tell them?" I looked at my grandma and grandpa.

A long look passed between them before Grandpa nodded. "Go ahead."

I related the woman's story, but not about the medicine. I told them of what happened to her and what I did to help my family. By now it was late, so Grandpa invited them all over to our place at sunrise tomorrow to finish this story. Everyone agreed, and we all left Joe's house. I walked with my grandparents, surprised when Jimmy spoke as we were walking a distance apart.

"I think it's pretty cool you made a journey before I did. I was going to do mine this summer."

I smiled and replied, "Something in me wanted to go first this spring."

"Cool, good night," he said heading for his house.

"Good night," I called after him.

My grandma smiled at my grandpa like they had a secret.

"Hey, I saw that," I said. They both laughed.

We got home and found Uncle eating dinner. "Where were you guys?"

"Crazy story," Grandpa said.

"Must be, I came home, and Mom had left everything on the stove." Uncle laughed and looked at us. "Hope everything is okay, you look tired

"We're all good, and thanks for finishing up dinner, it smells delicious," I said.

Grandma already dishing out for Grandpa and her. I grabbed a plate and ate. I was so hungry I went for a second plate.

"You must be growing," Uncle joked. I smirked at him and filled my plate. "I'm only 5-foot-three and not likely to grow anymore."

I enjoyed my meal, and then cleaned the kitchen. Everyone else headed for bed. Always up last, I thought. I finished the chores and crawled into bed. What a day. I grabbed my diary and started to write down what happened. Grandma knocked on my door and came in, she gave me a kiss and said goodnight. I smiled and kissed her back. She left the room, and I picked up my diary and wrote down everything that happened earlier. When I finished I turned out the light and went to sleep.

Chapter Fifteen

Day 15
I awoke to voices in the other room. Blinking sleep away, with bleary eyes, I checked the time. I was shocked to see it was 8:20am.

Oh my God! Are they all here already? I recognized the medicine man's voice and shoved myself out of bed. In a rush I brushed the tangles out of my hair and scrambled into my clothes. I took a few minutes to braid my hair and tie it up. I took a deep breath and opened my door.

Everyone looked up at me from the table where they were eating breakfast. A chorus of 'Good Morning' greeted me.

"She's been waking up later than eight since her journey," Grandpa says.

"She's gained some knowledge," Joe, the medicine man replied.

Grandma put a plate down on the table for me next to Grandpa and the elder. I offered a prayer then started to eat. Grandma brought me a coffee and I thanked her in our language rather than English. She smiled and stroked a hand down my hair.

A knock on the door interrupted our gathering. Grandma answered the door and invited the members of the family from last night into the kitchen. They filed in and Grandma offered them coffee and food. They declined, as they had already had breakfast, but they did accept some coffee.

I finished eating, hardly touching my meal. My stomach was knotted with nerves. Grandma removed my plate, and I got up to help clear off the table. The men talked about last night and the elder asked me to sit down with them and finish up the story from the evening before.

I joined them and then got up quickly. I needed to get my diary. After I retrieved the book from my room I sat down at the table again. I began to read what I'd written, starting from day one. I included all my dreams and visions except the teaching one. It was something shared with only me, and I felt it was too intimate and special to share with anyone other than Grandma. Plus I didn't want rumors going around that I was in league with a witch.

I related everything that happened to the woman, and when I was done, they all agreed that it was the same dream others had experienced.

"The stories that have been told and passed down say nothing of this woman, and no one has ever bothered to look into this further 'til now, thank you," the medicine man said, giving a short nod of his head at me.

Everyone at the table stared at me. Hand on my diary, I smiled. "It was nothing. I was only trying to find truth about the legend of the mountain, and why we were never allowed to travel so far up. I also wanted to help my grandpa"

The medicine man looked down at the table before he looked up again. "I was told never to journey in the mountains as a child, even though I heard the stories. I never disobeyed my father's wishes," he met my grandpa's gaze, "too chicken, we were," he joked.

Everyone laughed. Now we had an idea of what needed to be done. But the medicine man and the boy's vision were slightly different from mine. Maybe it was because I was her lover's bloodline? I shrugged off the notion. I couldn't wait to hear if anyone else was planning to do a journey now. After all, summer was so close, and the weather would be better than during my journey.

The boy and his father were silent, and the father didn't look well at all.

"How are you feeling?" Joe asked him.

The man replied, "I'm still weak and the dreams are still there. I feel as though I'm seeing things at times. I just need rest, I think."

I looked at my grandma and pulled her aside. "Should I do up some medicine for them?"

She looked worried and shook her head. "We should wait and ask Grandpa what to do. I don't want people thinking you have returned as a witch."

"Good point," I whispered. The village was too small, and if something like that got out, only the Creator knew what they could, or would, do to me. I was scared of banishment, the thought made me turn cold.

"Make some more tea and take it to the men," Grandma told me. While the water was boiling I glanced at the clock on the wall: 12:10pm.

The family of the sick man and boy agreed to take a trip into the mountains to see if they could get some answers of their own. The medicine man agreed to accompany them as he thought he might have to do the same thing to stop the dreams from coming to him.

* * *

That evening around 7:pm someone knocked on the door. Grandma opened it and invited the medicine man in.

"Can I have a copy of your map so we can find where these falls are in the mountains," Joe asked.

"Of course, I can draw it out. Oh yeah, and there's markers up there from where I marked my trail with ribbons," I said.

He grinned and laughed. "Well, you're a girl, easy for you to get lost."

I was annoyed but ignored the fact that both Joe and Grandpa laughed. I drew out the map I had in my diary and made them a copy.

"Well, that's it, that's where I went," I said, setting the paper down in front of Joe.

He looked at the map and his eyes got unfocussed. "I kind of remember this place with my mother, she used to take me and my sister up that way to pick plants."

I looked at him in amazement, then it dawned on me. The medicine man must be related, through his mother's bloodline, to one of the women who were cruel to the witch.

If that was so, everything was starting to make sense. The stories passed down among our people were wrong, and she was trying to tell her side of the story.

I looked at Grandpa. "What do you remember, or know about your father and grandfather?" I asked him.

He shook his head. "I can only remember small bits, but I have never heard anyone speak of this woman you see in your dreams."

I told him my thoughts on it all and he wanted to hear the story once more, but the way I would tell it, from my perspective rather than the dream woman's. So, I did, and it made more sense the way I told it.

I wrote out her story so the history of our village would reflect the truth. Even though it was a tragic event, it was a story that had to be told. She needed the truth to be told in order for her to be free from her rage of revenge.

So, I wrote her story. There wasn't a nice way to tell her story, but I felt she was urging me to speak for her. The feeling was so strong I couldn't ignore it. I wrote it out in my diary, and one day I would write this in our village history for other storytellers to tell and to know.

This is what I wrote:

She was raised in these mountains over a hundred years ago by her mother. A mother who was banished for being a healer and accused of being a witch The mother taught her daughter all that she could before she was banished from the village by the people of the settlement. At a very early age, the young girl met a friend, a boy from the village, and later they fell in love. His father told the young man he was forbidden to see the girl as she was born of a witch. But for years they met in the forest secretly. So deeply in love, the girl told him of her mother's banishment. The young boy promised to watch over her and that they would be together one day.

As they grew older, the boy became a man and was betrothed to another woman of his father's choosing. He broke off his long standing relationship with the now young woman. Her heart broke as she told him she was carrying his child. The man became someone she didn't recognize, he raged and yelled cruel accusations at her, before storming out of her hut.

Later that day, the chief, who was the young man's father, accused the heartbroken woman of being a witch and ordered her banished, just as her mother before her had been banished.

The village women came in a group, they burned her hut and took her to the falls far from the village. Here she would live. Unable to withstand the physical and emotional injuries inflicted by the group, she lost her unborn child. Overcome by rage and sorrow she welcomed the darkness that engulfed her soul and became a true witch. She cursed the group of women and all their offspring for all the generations to come. A curse on them that they and their descendants should live her pain and suffering over and over. She promised she would haunt them and their descendants until the wrongs done to her were set right. Until she was offered, and accepted, their apology and gave her forgiveness, they and all their offspring would go mad with a wasting sickness and die.

* * *

My heart slowed as I wrote the words. We needed to take responsibility for the wrongs done in the past and set things right. I thought I had made a good start. It felt right to tell her story, and I hoped that it would help ease her pain. This woman, my ancestor, was someone with a story that needed to be heard.

Sadness sat heavy on my heart as I closed my diary for the night.

"Time for bed," Grandma said, a hand on my shoulder.

I took my diary and got ready for bed, I crawled between the covers, turned out my lights, and said a prayer and then fell asleep.

Somehow, once again I knew I was dreaming, even though it felt so real and immediate.

I walked in the forest, wearing an all-white gown. The wind blew softly as I entered a clearing.

I recognized the place. It was the clearing up in the mountains. I had my arms stretched out on each side, touching the tall grass. At the other side of the clearing was the women. She was so beautiful, standing there, sun bright, flowers all over the place.

I walked toward her, and she smiled, her long, jet-black hair flowed in the wind like a raven's wing. When I reached her, a gentle smile touched her lips.

"Thank you for telling my story. But your journey hasn't ended, it's just beginning."

She bent down and picked some blooms from the flowers by her feet. "I'm not all bad, as some would have you believe. They just don't understand the gifts of knowledge from the plants and what nature has provided for us. We understand the plants because we listen to what the earth tells us. There is something in you that understands as well, you just need to explore and unlock your gift."

I shook my head in confusion. What did she mean?

"Your teacher will come soon." She turned and walked towards the trail to the falls, and I walked after her.

"What do you mean, my teacher?"

A playful smile crossed her face, and she blew the fluffy head of a dandelion at me and the fluff touched my cheeks like fairy dust. "Wake."

I opened my eyes and woke up. What did she mean by that? I sat up and looked at the time: 5:30am.

I heard my grandma cough in the kitchen, I got up and went to join her. She was having a drink, but she coughed again.

"Are you okay, Grandma?"

"Yes, yes. I just had the strangest dream though. I was walking in the forest, all dressed in white with feathers in my hair. I was beautiful and young again. I saw a beautiful woman in a wide green flower-covered field. The woman told me to watch over you and guide you to your teacher. She said she had sent someone, and I would know when she arrived." Grandma stopped and shook her head as if to make sense of the experience.

"Oh my God, Grandma. We had the same dream. What does it mean?"

"I don't know, but I believe there must be a healer coming to our village. Someone who can teach you what you must learn."

Dizziness swept over me, and I knew Grandma was with me in this vision. We saw a woman in a cloak, her face was covered. She wore a moose hide gown and feathers, a bag on her side with a staff in her hand, walking through the trees. Fog gathered all around and all we could see was her and the trees.

The vision ended at the same time for both of us and we clutched each other's hands.

"We must wake your grandfather at once," Grandma said, fear roughening her voice. She let go of my hands, rushed into their room and woke my grandpa. Once he woke, he sat up.

Grandma told him that we both had a vision, and that someone, a teacher, was coming to the village to seek us out. She went on to tell him about her dream and mine.

"We must be ready, just in case dream woman is the same as the one who sent her," Grandpa said, getting up.

"Who? A witch?" I looked at my grandpa and put my hand on his arm. "Don't worry,

Grandpa, whatever comes our way, good or bad, we have each other. Plus, it's just dreams and shadows of the stories of the last few nights."

Grandpa looked concerned. "Never-the-less, we should wait for the medicine man, Joe, to return from his journey and give us guidance. It's still earlier, go back to bed now."

It felt as if I'd just closed my eyes when the birds started chirping outside. Ugh. I rolled over with my head in the pillow and looked at the time: 7:30am. It sounded like everyone was already up. I sat up and looked around my room.

God, it was a mess, I'd better get it cleaned up so Grandma wouldn't have to. She was always cleaning, it seemed.

I stretched out, flipped my blanket off and reached over for the radio. I put on some tunes, country music from the 70's. I loved to listen to George Jones. My favorite was a song called, *The Likes of You*. I turned it up. Grandma opened my door.

"I hear you're up, would you like some coffee?"

"Yes, please." I got out of bed and started my tidying with the pile of dirty clothes in the corner. I moved them to my door. I didn't have a lot in my room, a dresser, a bed, and a trunk in the closet, along with a small table I put my radio on. I went to the kitchen, filled the mop bucket, and grabbed the broom.

Grandma smiled at me and handed me my coffee. "Cleaning time?"

I giggled. "Yes."

Back in my room, I moved everything around and washed the floor. Then I opened my window and let in the fresh air and took a deep breath in, letting out all my stress. I looked at the time when my cleaning was done: 9:05am. Not bad. My gaze fell on the trunk in my closet, I hadn't seen that thing in a very long time. I pulled it out, grunting because it was big and heavy. I opened the lid, just then Grandma came into my room.

"May I join you?"

"Sure."

She sat on my bed checked out my cleaning job. "I love what you did with your room." She grinned.

"I didn't want you to have to clean my room," I admitted.

"Thank you for that." She laughed.

I opened the trunk, inside there was some old mail, old pictures, and some other things wrapped up in hide. There was an old book, wrapped in what looked like cheese cloth. I picked up the pictures and Grandma looked over my shoulder.

"I was just a girl, and we took so many pictures of everything, even things that weren't important," Grandma said.

She looked through another stack of old photos and suddenly gave a tiny gasp when she came across a very old photo. She shivered and even I thought it gave off a creepy vibe.

"You okay?" Concerned, I touched her arm.

She nodded. "Yes." Her voice was a whisper.

I looked at the picture, it was an old, faded black and white picture of an old women standing outside a hut, all dressed in hide and feathers. To her left was a Raven.

"Who is she?"

"She was your great-great grandmother, who is not from these parts. She was from down river, a place called Riverside Village. That is where I am from too. Your grandfather and his father are from here, the mountains. I was married to him at age nineteen, and we have been together ever since. We had the most wonderful years exploring, before we settled down here to help his mother after his father got sick and passed with the madness."

"Huh." I couldn't think of anything else to say just then.

Grandma looked away for a second and changed the subject completely. I lifted the top layer of the trunk, and under it was a white gown with feathers and matching slippers. A tiny gasp passed my lips.

"It's so beautiful," I whispered, reaching out a hand but not wanting to actually touch it.

Grandma smiled. "That was my ritual gown, passed down to your mother." Beside the white dress was another beautiful dress made of hide. She held it up to admire it. "This was my mother's dress. My mother was a healer and it was required of the healer to wear your most beautiful hide when conducting the traditional ceremonies such as weddings. I wore this the day I married."

I tore my gaze away from the dress to look at her face. "Grandma, do you have a strong line of women healers in your family's bloodline?"

She looked at the window. "Yes."

"Why didn't you tell me we had healers in our family?" I was astounded she never shared that with me.

Grandma got up and moved to the window. "I didn't want you to try to do anything crazy, but you did anyways, you're just like your mother. Always asking questions, and soon you will leave me too." A sob shook her shoulders. I got up and hugged her.

"I love you. I will never leave you like that," I promised. I wiped the tears from her face, her wrinkled skin lined with memories of her long life. I kissed her cheek. "It's okay, Grandma," I said in our native tongue.

I turned away to give her a moment to compose herself. I folded the dresses, put them back, and closed the lid. I slid the trunk back in the closet and shut the door.

A few weeks passed with no sign of the teacher. The boy and his family returned with the medicine man from their journey. I was curious to know how things went, so I paid Joe a visit.

His wife greeted me when I knocked. "Joe isn't feeling well, maybe you should come back another day." She shut the door in my face.

Astounded, I stood looking at the door, lost for words. What was that all about? What happened on the journey? Was he mad at me? Did something go wrong?

I hurried down the narrow steps and went looking for my grandpa. I burst through the door.

"He won't see me," I blurted.

"Who?" Grandma asked.

"Joe, the medicine man."

Grandpa got up and put on his coat and hat. "He is the healer and guide of our dreams and journeys, he can't do that. He can't refuse to see you." Grandpa slammed the door and marched over to Joe's.

I looked out the window and watched Joe's door open and then Grandpa went in, the door closing behind him.

He'd been gone a few hours when someone knocked on our door. My cousins. Ash and Jimmy.

"Come in, but you can't stay long," Grandma told them.

They nodded and came into my room, closing the door behind them. Jimmy rolled a smoke.

"Did you hear how things went with their journey?" Ashton asked.

"No, what happened?" I sat at the edge of my bed.

"Word has it the old guy, Joe, had a vision and it scared him. And that family... They're okay now, something about some kind of ritual. Long story short, the family is good, but the old guy isn't," Jimmy said.

Leave it to Jimmy to sum things up quickly. I got up and took a drag off his smoke.

Grandma opened the door, interrupting us. "You boys must go. Grandpa is back." She shooed them out the door.

Grandpa called me over to join him at the table. Grandma sat next to him and held his hand. Grandpa looked concerned which made me uneasy.

"Joe had his journey, and everything was good. The women left them all alone, but then he had a vision. A vision of you and a woman in the woods. You were powerful and fought him, he said he always knew that you were a witch."

"What? No way, he probably mixed me up in his dreams because I was the one who gave him the map." My stomach dropped; fear mingled with anger. "How dare he accuse me of being a witch? What's next? Banishment?" I slammed my hand on the table, got up, went to my room and shut the door with a huge bang. I threw myself on the bed, crying with anger and frustration.

Grandpa gave a soft knock on my door and came in. He sat at the end of my bed, looking out the window. I sat up and wiped my eyes.

"I remember when your mom came home with you, you were a little bundle of pink faced joy wrapped in moose hide. Your mother put you on my lap, I held you and you looked up at me with those blue eyes and I knew the water ran deep in your eyes. You are strong and whatever kind of visions Joe may have had; I know you are a lot stronger than him. He has seen it, and he is scared. He will say things, but you must hold your tongue. Your grandma and I raised you from both sides of our village's bloodline. Be proud and never show them your anger."

I cried again and hugged him tightly. "Thank you, Grandpa."

Grandma opened the door and looked in. "You hungry?"

Grandpa nodded, got up, and kissed me on my head. "Don't worry, remember." He winked and left the room.

I wiped my tears and got ready for dinner. Time to eat and then story time before bed. After we ate, Grandpa sat by the fire and told his story of when he was a young father and took my uncle out for his first hunt. He laughed. Uncle didn't want to shoot the moose but tried to make friends with it. "You should have seen the look on his face when I had to shoot it for dinner," Grandpa said.

We all laughed. Uncle came out of his room and joined up. "The moose was cute, okay? he said in his own defense.

Everyone laughed harder. We had a snack and called it a night at 8: pm.

I dreamed again, and just like last time, I knew it was a dream.

I was wearing a gown, kind of like the one in the trunk, but different. My feathers were white, not black or grey, bright white like a light. I was holding a baby fox that was hurt. I healed him and he ran around me. I could hear his voice in my head. He said, "Thank you, beautiful healer." Then he ran through the tall grassy meadow. I touched the grass and pulled out the water bag by my side and washed my hands. I could still feel the cool fresh water running over my hands as I woke. I held my hands up, the water felt so real, but my skin was dry. Why did weird things have a way of seeming natural at 3:30 in the morning? I grabbed my diary and scribbled down everything I could remember so I could tell my grandma in the morning. Closing the book, I rolled over and went back to sleep.

A raven squawked loudly at my window. I opened my eyes just in time to see him fly away. *Weird, why squawk at me and then just fly away?*

It was time to get up, I stretched my back out and yawned. Uncle's voice came from the kitchen, he must have returned from his trap lines which he visited early in the morning. I jumped up and stuck my head out the door. He was at the table sipping coffee. I hurried across the floor and hugged him,

"Good morning, sprout. Grab a coffee, I just got home, now I have to unload the sled and haul everything in. Want to help?"

I jumped as if I was 10 years old again, I loved helping Uncle. I ran to my room, closed the door and pulled on my clothes. I just put my hair in a bun, and I was ready.

Grandpa laughed at me when I rushed back into the kitchen. "Ha, look who just wants dried meat so bad," he teased me.

"Yes, that's me," I replied.

Everyone started to laugh now. I was just reaching for my coffee cup, when my sight when white and I fell into a vision.

She was here! Walking through the village, down the road, wearing a cloak and her face was covered. I couldn't see what she looked like, my heart pounded hard like the beat of the drums. The woman was wearing a beautiful dress like mine in the dream from last night. Her feathers were grey and white, she carried a bag at her side and matching shoes. The feathers on her staff fluttered in the breeze as she headed toward my street. I saw my house through her eyes. She was coming...

I shook my head to clear my eyes and blinked. My uncle was holding my hand with Grandma by my side. Grandpa was standing over us. They were yelling at me to wake up. Their combined gasp of relief was clearly audible when I took a deep breath in.

"She is here," I yelled. I came back to myself lying on the floor.

My uncle was confused. "What the hell just happened to her?" he shouted.

Grandma replied, "She had a vision."

"A vision? A vision that just knocks her out like that must be one heck of a vision," he was still yelling. He got to his feet and went to stare out the window.

Grandpa helped me up to get up and I stood for a moment to clear my head. Without warning, a sharp pain lanced straight through my temple, from left to right. I closed my eyes as tight. I could hear Grandma looking for some medicine. Uncle helped me to the chair, and I sank down into it. Grandma brought me two of the pills the doctors gave her when they were last here. She pressed a cup of water into my hand. I swallowed the pills, emptying the cup.

Someone knocked on the door and I opened my eyes. Grandpa opened the door, and I could see who stood there. It was her. The teacher. She had arrived!

* * *

Grandma welcomed the woman in. She stood in the door, cloak covering the opening. She stepped in and apologized for the sudden intrusion, then said, I think you knew I was coming, and you all know why I am here!

She removed her cloak and reveled her face, she was a woman about 40 years of age and the white in her hair said she was full of wisdom. The teacher was nice looking, strong, appearing as if she could fight off, or take down, a bear! Her voice was stern and authoritative, I could tell she had taught a lot before. She came in and sat down, Moonlight offered her a drink. She accepted the coffee and looked around the house.

"Where are the other two?"

I looked at Grandma and shrugged my shoulders in an 'I don't know' motion.

The teacher spoke in her stern voice. "Sorry, but there are three students in my visions."

As she finished speaking there was a knock on the door. Grandma opened it to find two families waiting outside. She invited them all in and we all gathered in the living room. I had seen the people before in the village, but we'd never spoken much, just a friendly hello when we passed by each other.

Everyone was introduced as my grandparents knew them. Everyone shook hands and murmured greetings. There were two other girls who were my age with their parents.

The first girl said, "I'm Tall Girl."

The second girl said, "I'm Small Girl."

I smiled and said, "I'm Go'diah."

The teacher asked me and the girls to wait outside while she talked with the parents. We went outside and waited on the top step. There was an awkward silence as we stood there, as if none of us knew what to say.

I looked around and decided to break the silence. I cleared my throat. "So, are you girls having dreams or visions too?"

They looked at each other then back at me. Something passed between them, and they nodded to each other as if they had come to a silent agreement.

"Yes, to both!" they said almost in unison.

"Are you the girl that went on a journey quest alone?" Tall Girl asked.

"Yes, did it in ten days!" I said proudly.

"Were you scared to be alone out there on the mountain in the woods all by yourself?" Small Girl inquired.

I smiled and replied, "Yes, at first. But I had Midnight with me, my dog!" I pointed at him where he was tied up and laying down minding his own business.

The girls smiled at him and he thumped his tail.

"Did you have any visions of the mountain?" Small Girl asked.

I answered as best I could. "I'm not sure, just dreams, by the falls where I was camped."

The door opened, interrupting us. The girls' parents came out and took the girls home. I waved at them as they left.

The teacher stepped out. "Good night, I will see you early tomorrow." She went down the steps and headed over to the medicine man's house.

Oh, boy, I thought as the teacher knocked on Joe's door. Grandma opened the door behind me.

"Get inside, now." She moved toward the living room, expecting me to follow.

I turned and went in quickly. Uncle, Grandpa, and Grandma were all standing in the living room waiting for me.

"Sit down," Grandpa said. I knew by the tone he was worried.

Uncle looked pale as though he'd heard something scary. Worry mixed with fear built in my gut. I sat down beside Grandma and waited for Uncle and Grandpa to sit.

Grandpa cleared his voice before he spoke. "You and the two other girls have been chosen to go to the mountains with this teacher for ten days of learning. Without markers, you must follow her to the place your visions began, to the falls. You must also bring a gown, as it is a part of the ritual. You are to wear it during your teaching. Grandma will give you your mother's one. There, in the mountains, you will learn from the teacher and be tested," he paused an expression of pride in me crossing his face, "if you are successful you will become the next medicine women of our village! But beware, some have been overcome by this testing. A person can lose their mind if they are not careful. The three of you will all be tested again when you return and stand against the medicine man himself for the title. Remember, he has practiced many moons and was taught by his grandmother, and mother. Caution must be taken if your journey leads you down this path."

I looked over at Uncle, he had his head down and looked worried. Grandma was praying, her lips moving silently.

"You must be up at five in the morning and be ready to leave at first light which should be around six am. You can only bring a small pack of essential things you will need for the ten days you are gone. Mother Nature will provide the rest."

"What?" Shock rooted me to the spot. "So, no extra gear?"

Grandpa nodded. "No."

"What about a tent?" I persisted. How was I supposed to survive on the mountain without a tent?

"No!" Grandpa would not change his mind or go against the teacher's orders.

"So, what should I pack then?"

Grandma lifted her head. "Just a week's worth of clothes, your parka and sleeping bag."

I sighed with disappointment and looked at everyone. "Do I have to go?" It didn't seem like such an adventure anymore.

"Yes, you have no choice. You were chosen, and you must never question the path our Creator laid out for us. You will make your family proud, and our bloodline well remain strong in the village, you must go," Grandpa said, his face solemn.

"Okay, I guess I really don't have a choice," I agreed with some reluctance.

"You must eat first, I will help you pack once we've done eating," Grandma said.

She cooked us a nice meal and I ate until my stomach hurt. Who knew when I would get food this good again. When everyone was done I helped Grandma clean up. She followed me into my room and helped me pack. When we came back into the living room I stood while Grandpa saged me and prayed for my journey.

Uncle rolled me a smoke and lit it. "Let's smoke before you go."

I joined him on the porch. We sat outside, side by side, and watched the moon come up.

"Not full yet," he said, and handed me the smoke so I could take a drag.

I looked over at Midnight. "Will you watch over Midnight for me while I'm gone?"

I glance at Uncle from the side of my eye. "Uncle, I'm scared. What if I don't pass the test?"

He pulled me in for a hug and patted my back.

"Of course I will look after your dog. You got this. It's just a journey, and I know you well do good and make us proud," he encouraged me.

I hugged him back.

He released me and got to his feet, reaching down a hand to pull me up too. "Better go to bed, you'll need the rest for the hike."

We went inside and everyone went to bed.

Part Two

Shúhta Dene
Bloodline

Chapter One

The Mountain Journey Begins
Day 1

Five a.m. arrived far quicker than I wanted. I hardly slept, I so nervous about this trip I rolled out of bed and got dressed. When I went to the kitchen Grandma, Uncle and Grandpa were all sitting at the table having a coffee. I walked over, poured a cup, went to join them.

Grandpa said, "I put some tobacco in your bag in case you want to smoke."

I hugged him hard, trying to swallow the sob that felt like a lump in my throat.

"I'm scared, Grandpa," I whispered.

He looked at me with a tear in his eye and patted my hand. "It's going to be okay, you are our little sprout. You well do fine, we are all so proud of far you come. Always remember Grandma, Uncle and me well be right here waiting when you return."

He hugged me and Grandma leaned in for a group hug.

Grandma said, "Come have something to eat. The walk is going to be long and you need your strength."

I smiled softly at her and sat down at the table to get a bite of breakfast. I looked at the time. It was 5:40am almost time to meet the teacher and the other girls. I looked out the window at the blue black sky; the sun was coming soon. As I got my jacket and shoes on Uncle looked over at me.

"You better come back a medicine woman or you'll sleep with Midnight outside," Uncle teased me with a laugh in his voice.

I laughed back at him. "Cheeky!"

I looked out the window and saw that Teacher was heading over from Joe's house. My heart pounded, ricochetting off my ribs. She knocked on our door and entered without waiting for Grandma to open it for her.

She looked at me up and down before she spoke. "You ready?"

I nodded that I was, somehow I couldn't say the words. She headed outside so I grabbed my pack and followed her. We stood at the bottom of the steps and I gave my family a hug. When I stepped back I could see the two girls from last night with their families coming down the road. Soon we would all be here and ready for our journey. The girls' families hugged them, and the group of us set off to the trail with Teacher in the lead.

We walked half the day before partway up the trail Teacher stopped.

"We should rest a bit," she said after taking a look around.

Us three girls threw our packs on the ground and sat down. I pulled out my water container while the girls did the same. I had a drink and looked around. The sun was up and shining brightly. I looked at my watch to check the time: 10:am.

Teacher noticed what I'd done and walked over to me. "What was that?" she demanded radiating disapproval.

I looked up at her in confusion. "Huh? My water?"

She glared down at me. "What did you just look at?"

I said, "My watch!"

"Hand it over," she said, her tone dripping with disgust. She turned to the other girls. "Do either of you have a watch too?"

They looked at each other uncertainly before answering. Both girls admitted they did have a watch.

"Give them to me." Teacher held out her hand.

I handed her my watch and so did the other girls. Teacher put them in her bag.

"You will learn to tell time without things such as this," she glanced upward at the sun, "it's 10:am. We must move on."

My mouth fell open in shock, how did she know the time? I looked at the sun and was lost for the answer. We hit the trail in a single line, and she was way ahead of us moving at a brisk pace. We got to the first camp site, the sun was lower in the sky but I had no idea what time it was without my watch.

Teacher waited for us to catch up and came over to us. We will make camp here for the night."

I was tired and feeling a bit angry at how she was treating us. I said Huh!! in my head carefully not looking at her in case my expression gave me away.

Without any hesitation, she turned to me. "I heard that!" She moved past me her whole body rigid with disapproval.

I was shocked again. How did she know what I thought? No way, she couldn't have heard me, I didn't say anything out loud, only in my head. Maybe my face did give me away. I shrugged it off then pulled out my sleeping bag. I laid down on it relieved to ease my aching muscles. The other two girls did the same.

Teacher frowned at us. "Get up, gather the wood, quickly, it's not going to gather itself." She sat on a log and watched us.

I got up in a huff, annoyed and resenting her tone of voice. I scrounged through the surrounding trees and started to pick up wood, deadfall and some grass and leaves we could use for kindling. The girls did the same. While we gathered up the wood and piled it at the campsite, she just sat there watching us.

I looked at her when I dropped my last armful of wood. "Okay what now?" I let my tone resonate with condescension.

Teacher stood up and moved toward me. I stood my ground although tremors of uneasiness snaked up my back.

"Do you speak to your elders this way?" She stopped in front of me.

I looked at her stern face and embarrassment swept through me.

"Well," she demanded.

I paused and shuffled my feet like did when I was a child got into trouble. "No," I admitted with my head down. From the corner of my eye I saw Small Girl smirking at me. Tall Girl just looked afraid.

"Step aside, out of my way," Teacher said.

I Moved back a few paces, and she bent over and started the fire. A nice and strong fire burned brightly in the ring of stones.

"Tonight, we rest and eat, prepare for tomorrow. We will arrive at the falls by tomorrow's sundown," Teacher told us.

We all got a snack out of our packs and ate what we brought with us. As I laid there in my sleeping bag, I thought to myself, well I'm back and sooner than I thought. But this time around, it's not for the same reason, or a relaxing trip as I planned for when I came back this way. I looked up at the stars and saw the dipper. I missed my Grandpa but kept in mind why I was here once again, I closed my eyes and fell asleep.

* * *

It was foggy everywhere, so thick I couldn't see a thing. Another dream: seems like all I do on the mountain is have weird dreams and visions.

Then I could see the teacher through the fog. She was lost and yelling for help but there was no one around. I woke up abruptly to hear the fire crackling loudly. The fire was bigger than when I went to sleep. I rolled around to look, and Teacher was sitting by the fire with her legs crossed, hands on her knees, eyes closed. I paid no attention to what she was doing and rolled over to go back to sleep. I thought to myself, well she's got this. The dream didn't seem important. I didn't know this woman and it was probably because we just met that she was in my dream. I went back to sleep.

Day 2
Respect

Morning came with an icy breath. I was freezing lying on the cold ground event through my sleeping bag. I got up quick and shook off my sleeping bag. Look around the campsite, I saw that the two girls were still sleeping, but Teacher was nowhere to be seen. The fire had gone down to glowing embers so put more wood on and stirred it up. The other two girls blinked sleep from their eyes and sat up.

"Where's the teacher?" Small Girl asked.

I shrugged my shoulders and looked in my pack for the small pot I knew was there. Grandma packed me coffee and I really needed some this morning. The two girls got out of their sleeping bags and moved to stand close to the fire.

"Wonder where she went?" Tall Girl said.

"Think she left us?" Small Girl looked scared, "she can't just leave us out here, can she?" Worry creased her face as she kept looking around. The fire got hot enough so took out my water container and poured it in the small pot with some coffee grounds and set the pot on a stone in the hot coals. The girls looked very uneasy, jumping every time the fire snapped.

"Were you scared up here when you were here alone?" Small Girl asked.

Of course, I was, but I leaned over to pick up a stick before I replied. "I learned to overcame my fear that's all, and once I did that there was nothing to fear."

Just then the teacher came out of the woods with three fresh rabbits. I was shocked again, but I didn't say a word, just smiled at her.

She threw the rabbits down by the fire and asked in a disappointed way, "Do you know how to clean them?"

"Yes." All three of us said in unison.

Teacher knelt by the fire warming her hands. "Have any of you two girls ever been in the mountains before this?"

Both Small Girl and Tall Girl shook their heads to indicate they hadn't.

Teacher gazed at our surrounding for a moment. "These mountains are sacred grounds, they keep us safe, and the energy speaks to us here. You must learn to listen to it in these woods." She got to her feet and grabbed the rabbits. "Come," she said, "clean these rabbits because we must go soon."

The sun was rising, and the birds were out, we skinned the rabbits, one each. I wrapped up the remains in the pelt and washed off my hands. Teacher was sitting in silence watching us. The girls staking their rabbits to cook by the fire as I walked off toward the forest with my bundle in my arms.

"Where are you going?" Tall Girl sounded puzzled and worried.

I turned around. "Getting rid of the remains."

She looked at me like I was weird. "My dad just makes the fire real big, throws them in and burns it all."

I shook my head and smiled. "Why burn them when you can provide something back to nature?" I walked into the forest and buried the remains deep. I listened to the wind blowing softly through the trees on my way back. I came back to the campfire, the teacher hadn't moved from where she was sitting but she smiled at me and nodded.

She checked the rabbits over the fire, mine is there too. "They're doing good, a little bit more and they'll be done." She sat back down and watched while I sat and dug out my tobacco and rolled a smoke.

"Why do you smoke that?" Teacher asked.

I looked at her and thought before I replied. "I guess it helps my nerves calm down when I am nervous."

Teacher looked at the sky as if I hadn't spoken. "We must go soon. By the sun it is close to 9:30."

I looked at the sun and the sky and wondered how she was doing that. What did she see that I didn't? I shook my head and packed up my pack. The rabbits were done, we give thanks and eat. The skin all crispy on the outside and the meat tender and juicy on my tongue. Then it was time to go, the teacher put out the fire and made sure we left nothing to indicate we had been there.

We headed out with Teacher in the lead, and I was at the back as the two girls walked between us. We have been walking for at least a good half a day, when I decided look at the position of the sun. It was now just between the middle of the sky and the tree line. I made a guess that it was around 2 or 3 in the afternoon. Maybe that was Teacher's secret to telling time. I made a note to keep track of the sun's path across the sky. My back was sore and we were slowing down in our pace.

Teacher looked back at us. "We rest here and then we go again."

The three of us were tired, and the hikes up the hills were hard on all of us, except Teacher or so it seemed. I threw my pack on the ground and dropped down on it.

"My back." My whining set the other two off. They started complaining about their legs and their backs and how long this hike was.

Teacher frowned;, disappointment etched in her features. She got to her feet and regarded us. "You girls whine like puppies looking for their mother," she said in disgust. "Look around, where do you think we are?"

The girls put their heads down in submission. I looked at her, stood up in frustration and snapped at her even though Grandpa always warned me I should learn to hold my tongue and my temper. "Listen, we didn't ask to be here, and we didn't ask to come with you. It's all because of these visions and dreams, so sorry if were slowing you down. These girls have never been in the woods before this and you expect them to just know it all and keep up with you?" I was angry and I let it show.

Teacher stepped close to me, I could feel her strength pushing at me, but I held my ground.

"I did not choose to come and teach a bunch of little babies be healers. It is my destiny, and you must learn to hold your tongue in my presence," she yelled, her voice echoing even in the forest.

The look in her eyes said it all, I sat back down in silence, no longer challenging her. She looked at the sun. "We must go."

I sighed and grabbed my pack. The girls got up and we all headed up the trail. The sun was just above the tree line, and I could see all the ribbons I had marked my trail with earlier in the year. Yup, I was back. It wasn't too much longer before we got to the clearing where Midnight and I had camped. We moved past it and onto the trail, then through the forest and the vines, until we came to the falls.

Both girls gasped with amazement. It really was so beautiful, even though I had seen it before it still struck me. The rushing sound of the water was making me thirsty. I took my cup out of my pack, dipped it in the fresh water and had a nice mouth full. The teacher walked over to the other side of the pool of water at the base of the falls and looked around. She came back around to stand beside me. "Show me your camp that I have heard of. Where you camped here before."

I picked my pack up and headed to the other side through the bushes while she followed me. The fishing line I made to hang my clothes on, the bark looking slab I made a little table out of, it was still there. Teacher looked at it all and smiled not quite hiding her amazement.

"You did good here," she said. She inspected the dugout I made for my fire, she nodded with approval. "I need to look at you more closely," she said, looking into my face for moment. She moved over to look at my old wood pile. Small Girl and Tall Girl were standing beside not sure what to do.

"Start a fire, Tall Girl," she orders.

"You, go fish and catch our dinner," she tells Small Girl.

Both girls went to do what she asked. I waited for her to tell me what she wanted me to do. I stood silent while she set up her pack and pulled out her rolled up hide. I grabbed my pack and looked at her.

"Why we couldn't have at least brought tents for cover if it rains?" I asked in a very quiet voice.

She looked at the fire and smiled. "do you think hundreds of years ago we had tents out here?"

"Well, no," I replied.

Teacher looked at the heavens. "We slept under the stars, we had nothing but what Mother Nature provided for us," she kept her eyes on the fire, "she provides, shelters from the rain, food for our bellies, water to nourish our thirst, medicine to heal our sick. She is our mother and there is nothing that she can't provide for us out on her lands."

I looked at her with a tiny smile on my face. "Okay but if it rains, you can't say I didn't suggest tents." My tiny smile widened into a cheeky grin.

Teacher smiled back. "We shall see."

Small Girl came back from the pool just then with empty hands. "I can't find any fish, if they're there they aren't biting."

Teacher shook her head in disbelief and got up. "You both come with me, I will teach you how to fish." She called Tall Girl to join them.

Both girls looked at me. "Why doesn't she have to do anything?" she complained.

Teacher regarded them sternly. "Did either of you girls make a journey here by yourself? Now why would I ask her to do the same things she has already done on her first journey here? She know these things, but you two need to learn them as well."

Both girls put their heads down and followed her to the water.

The teacher showed them how to catch fish. I came along to just watch and be companiable. I sat on the rocks by the lake and watched her teach them. I realized that she was a good teacher. After about half an hour the girls finally caught two fish. They were both so excited it reminded me of Midnight, him splashing in the water and playing with a fish. I giggled softly. I missed my dog.

The lesson was over, teacher and the girls were done fishing now. We all made out way back to the camp. The sun had moved below the tree line, it was getting chilly in the air. We got back to the camp and I fed the fire right away without being told to. Teacher asked the girls to clean the fish which they did with no problem. We cooked them up over the fire and enjoyed a nice bite to eat. Teacher made sure the girls went and buried the guts away from out camp. I was full and tired now while we sat by the fire. Teacher looked at the moon and stirred. "We must sleep now, your training of the herbs well start early tomorrow morning." She put more wood on the fire as we all got into our sleeping bags and fell asleep.

Chapter Two

Day 3
First day of teaching, the plants

It was cold when I woke up, the air so chilly I could hear the trees stretching out their branches with tiny creaks and snaps. I sat up and just listened. The ground started warming under me. I could feel the shift in the climate as the trees got ready for the sunbeams to slant down and meet their embrace. Something was different today. I didn't understand what was happening, but I seemed strangely connected to the earth and the area around me. I closed my eyes and listened with my heart; it was a feeling I couldn't describe if someone had asked me to. Tickling lights, peace, serenity. I opened my eyes to see the teacher staring at me.

"What do you feel? she asked.

I looked up at her. "Peace! Serenity!"

"Do you hear the earth waking?"

"Yes." The word burst out of me.

"What do you hear when you close your eyes?

I closed my eyes and listened quietly. "I hear the trees stretching their branches, I hear the small bush shaking in the wind, shedding the frost left from last night. I can hear the leaves open as the sun hits them." I opened my eyes and met her gaze.

"Very good." Teacher smiled.

The other two girls stirred in their sleeping bags, rolled over and sat up. Tall Girl rubbed her eyes and looked at Teacher and me with suspicion lurking behind her eyes.

"What did we miss? What have you been doing while we slept?" Tall Girl crawled out of her sleeping bag.

"Nothing at all, were just waking up, you girls should do the same." Teacher moved to poke up the fire.

Small Girl got up too and we all gathered for the breakfast Teacher was making for us. After breakfast we cleaned up and waited for instructions.

Teacher looked up at the sun that was starting its daily journey across the sky. "Girls, get into the gowns you brought. Your teaching begins with the plants and how they can help us. Meditation will be the remainder of today's lesson. Now go and prepare yourselves."

Tall Girl and Small Girl got their packs while Teacher went behind a bush to change into her teaching gown. The girls took out their lovely white gowns and went off to find a spot to change. I stood by myself by the fire awash in confusion. Shaking myself into action, I pulled out the gown my grandma had packed for me. My mother's gown. I lifted it and held it up to the light. It was beautiful. *My mom wore this at my age? I wonder if she had to go through this teaching too? Or am I the first?*

I decided I would ask Grandma when I got home. Just then the teacher stepped out of the trees. Instead of the clothes she wore normally, she was clad in a white and silky gown that flowed down to her feet. Matching slippers peeked out from under the hem. She looked different in it, it was like she glowed in the sun.

She glanced over at me where I was still standing holding my mother's gown in front of me. "Why aren't you dressed yet?"

Before I could answer her, the girls came out of the bushes. They were wearing beautiful gowns as well.

"Do you not understand what we are doing? Or what the gowns mean?" A confused frown wrinkled Teacher's forehead. "How about you two?" She turned to the other two girls who both indicated they had no idea. Teacher threw her arms in the air, turned away from us and said something in her tongue I didn't understand. She put her hands on her hips, turned back to us and stared in disbelief. "This is going to take all day," she said sounding annoyed and disappointed. "You," she pointed at me, "go get your gown on and meet us by the falls. You two," she waved at the girls, "follow me."

They disappeared in the direction of the waterfall. Frustrated, I yanked off the clothes

I'd slept in and wriggled into the gown and slippers. I shivered, the air was still a bit cold to be running around in these gowns. I found the trail and walked towards the falls.

The teacher was standing by the falls in the rocks when I arrived. They all turned toward me.

"You look beautiful," Teacher tells me.

I kept my expression from giving away how I really felt. "Thanks," I said but couldn't keep the bite of annoyance out of my voice. I could tell she heard it, but must have decided to let it slide. She led us to the deep part of the forest where everything had happened on my solitary journey. I followed at the end of the line as memories of my journey came flooding back like the waters that flowed through the mountains. The trail was a different way from the one I had taken. Teacher seemed to know where to go without using any markers. I was lost, I had never been this far into the forest. We got to an open meadow where there were so many plants it looked like a garden. Berries here and there, flowers of all sorts, grass, herbs of different kinds. It was beautiful and I breathed in all the mingled scents as we walked to the center and stopped.

Teacher turned around. I glanced up at the sun which was now a quarter of the way up the sky. I'd been practicing telling the time by the sun so, I figured it was maybe around 10:am. Teacher began to tell us why the gowns were so important and why we needed to wear them as we learned. She spoke of how the white stands for purity; how when we wear the gown during our teachings we can find the energy in all things. The gown is only passed down, or created specially, for those of the bloodline of healers. Each is a special gown meant only for us. I let her words flow over me and started to understand the importance of the gown. I ran my hands down the material, smoothing it over my hips. The other girls were smiling and preening and admiring their dresses.

The teacher began walking with us following. She moved through the field naming the plants and giving us the meaning of the names and what each can do for us. I tried my best to remember the names: ginger root, bay leaves, aloe vera, sweet grass, basil, sage, dandelions, peace lilies, white orchid, red flowers, baby's breath, licorice root, rosemary, poison berries, thyme, herbs and so many others I couldn't keep track of.

She bent and picked a leaf from a plant by her feet, holding it up for us to see. "Basil is a very good one to use for curing sore stomachs. The leaves contain a high amount of linoleic acid which has anti-inflammatory properties. Licorice root tea helps relieve digestive symptoms also."

I was so surprised, I never realized there was so much to learn about herbs and flowers and how much they could help us.

The teacher looked at the position of the sun. " Come, it's time to take a break and get something to eat. Let all that information settle in your brains."

We were all quiet on the walk back to camp. When we got there, we all sat down around the fire. I was tired but excited by what I had learned and the prospect of all that I still had to learn. Small Girl and Tall Girl huddled together muttering under their breath.

"I'm really not into all this weird stuff and traipsing through the bush," Small Girl whispered.

"I'm not either, but my parents insist that I should do this and bring honor to our family. I guess I don't have to like it, but my father would be furious if I refused," Tall Girl whispered back.

I quit listening to their complaints and concentrated on remembering the names of the plants Teacher showed us and what each plant offered us. The teacher ignored them as well. She dug in her pack, pulled out some food and settled down to eat. I followed her example and after a bit the other girls did too. When we were finished we cleared up any mess and waited for Teacher to speak.

"Now, we need to do some meditation to get connected to the energy of the land, and learn to listen. You girls need to learn this more than anything," Teacher said getting to her feet. "Come, let's go."

We followed her again back through the trail on the dark side of the falls where she led us into the forest until we came to a small clearing. A jolt of astonishment shot through me. I recognized this place from my vision. It was where the woman taught me and her daughter about the flowers to help my grandpa. I smiled and let my shoulders relax. This was a good place.

"Have you been here before? You look as if you have seen this place before," Teacher asked, her eyes steady on mine.

I nodded, indicating that I knew this place.

"When may I ask?"

In a quiet voice I told her of my vision.

Teacher smiled. "She comes to see me and guides me in my dreams, that is what led me to seek out you all. She found me in a dream, the wise healer asked me to find the missing three, to teach and restore what once was the balance," her voice was soft as she spoke.

I smiled in understanding. The other two girls' shocked faces mirrored each other.

"We've both had those dreams, she has come to us as well. That's how we knew that someone was coming to teach us. We never thought she was visiting other people too," Tall Girl said.

"Now, remove your slippers and close your eyes. Breathe in all the beauty around you, take in all the good energy and let out all your doubts and fears. Let go of all the negative energy that holds you back, weighs you down," her voice was soft and almost mesmerizing.

I let my bare feet sink into the earth, the warm energy flooding up my legs and through my body. I threw my head back and let the dance of the leaf shadows cast by the sunbeams sweep over me. We stood for a while in silence.

"Can we sit down?" Tall Girl broke the quiet of the clearing.

"Yes, sit," Teacher sounded annoyed.

I sank down onto the forest loam, with my eyes closed, crossing my legs. The trees whispered around us, I breathed in and out, conscious of the air in my lungs, relaxing, bringing in positive energy and letting go of any negativity with each outward breath. With spurt of joy, I realized I was starting to feel the earth, feel everything around me. The energy flowing through every root and leaf. Everything was connected, the grass, the plants, the flowers, the bushes, my body, everything was moving and flowing with nature. The earth, the sky, the water...

A loud sneeze shocked me out of my trance. I opened my eyes to see the teacher who looked a bit annoyed. She tipped her head back to gaze up at the sky before she turned her attention to us.

She quizzed the other two girls about the plants from earlier, but didn't single me out. I sat quiet, and listened.

"How do you feel about what you let go and left behind when you meditated just now?" She looked at each of us in turn.

The question took me by surprise, and I had to mull it over in my mind. The silence in the clearing was broken only by bird song.

Finally, Tall Girl spoke, "I didn't feel much, just heard the birds, it made me so relaxed, I wanted to sleep." She giggled.

Small Girl grinned and gave a tiny laugh. "I felt the ground moving from under me."

"Very good." She smiled at Small Girl and turned to me.

"I felt that everything was connected, that we are one with nature. It was good to let all the frustration and anger of out of me," I said, trying to explain the enormity of the experience.

Teacher looked impressed and nodded. "Now, it is time to go, we must get dinner and call it a night. But first we thank our mother for the day." She bent her head and each of us said some words of thanks before gathering our things and heading back to camp. When we got back to the camp I was exhausted. Almost as if the earth had taken some of my energy.

The teacher brought some bread out. "There is enough for each of you to take a loaf and eat it all. Meditation takes up some of our energy and you need to replenish it."

I took mine and stuffed pieces into my mouth. It felt like I hadn't eaten in a month. The other girls were doing the same thing.

After a few minutes I felt much better. I got up and grabbed my pack to change into normal clothes and put my parka on as it was getting chilly. The two girls did the same. Teacher started the fire and went to change into some normal clothes.

"I'm off to get some rabbits for dinner, you girls wait here and keep the fire going hot," Teacher said and then disappeared into the forest,

I was still hungry so I took out some of the food still in my pack, the other girls grab must have been hungry too because they were snacking as well. I was glad Grandma packed me a lot of food. I love her so much. There were apples, carrots, Bannock, dried meat, coffee grounds with the mixings, and some dried fruits. I took some dried meat and a piece of Bannock, that was good enough for now. I put more wood on the fire and waited for the teacher to return. They sky was darkening; it was getting a bit late and there were still no signs of her. I started to worry maybe she had gotten lost while hunting. I looked across the fire to ask the other girls what they thought but they'd fallen asleep. I stiffen at the sound of something moving in the trees, it was getting closer... I waited, my heart started to pound. Maybe it was that bear again I scared off when I was up here last... Fear swept over me as the bushes moved in the firelight. I looked across at the sleeping girls...couldn't they hear it? They never moved and I was afraid to say anything. The bushes moved and Teacher stepped out into the firelight. I took a deep breath and exhaled.

"You scared me half to death," I cried. My heart was slowing down now.

Teacher threw three rabbits on the small table I made, then sat down by the fire.

"Why were you afraid?"

"There was bear around here when I camped before with my dog. I had to scare it off with a gunshot," I told her.

"Okay, then," she nodded, "get some sleep. I'll hand the rabbits up high in the trees and we can have them for breakfast."

"Okay." I crawled into my sleeping bag and even though I thought I wouldn't I fell asleep quickly.

Chapter Three

Day 4
Vision Quest

When we woke up Teacher brought down two of the rabbits and we cooked them over the fire for breakfast. The other rabbit, we saved for dinner leaving it up in the tree and out of reach of the bear if he was still hanging around. We finished eating but before I got up to help clean the campsite Teacher stopped me.

"What are each of you afraid of in these woods? On this mountain?"

I replied quickly without skipping a beat, "Bears and wolves."

The other two girls agreed.

Teacher stood up. "Today you will learn spiritual visions, that is when you see through the animals' eyes. Once you have mastered this, you can then talk to the animal through a spiritual connection you open with them when your minds meet. It is not an easy thing to learn, but it be done if you listen and concentrate, open your mind. This is a test to see if you have vision, let's go."

As we headed out, I was full of curiosity. Was it really possible? And if it was, I couldn't wait to get home and talk to Midnight and tell my grandparents. My body hummed with excitement. Our path took us up the mountain. Oh wow, I thought, we're heading up. I looked back, and there were just bushes.

"How far up are we going?"

She didn't answer me, but just kept walking. We hiked a long way up the mountain finally got to a nice spot where she stopped. There were birds everywhere, flying all around us, it was beautiful. Teacher noticed there was one bird who was hurt.

"Perfect." She went over and gently picked up the injured bird. One wing was hanging at an odd angle, it looked broken. She came back to us and put the bird gently in her pocket softly. We walked a little while longer and came to the edge of a cliff. It overlooked the whole valley. It is beautiful and green as far as I could see.

"Gather 'round me," she said sitting on the ground.

We sat down in a circle around her and she put the bird down. The poor thing chirped and held its wing out awkwardly.

"This part of the teaching will take most of the day, but we're all going to stay in this spot until all, or even one of you, manages a vision."

The girls and I looked at each other and shrugged our shoulders.

"Guess so," Tall Girl said, "I'll go first."

The teacher smiled. "I want you to clear your mind, meditate and concentrate on the bird. Try to feel what the bird is feeling, and make a connection to join with him, see through his eyes."

Tall Girl nodded and started with deep breathing, slow...in and out... and stared at the bird a very long time.

"Are you getting anything?" Teacher asked after a long time had passed.

Tall Girl sighed. "No. I'm trying, but I'm not getting anything."

"Can I try next?" Small Girl asked.

"Of course, give it a try. Do you remember what I told Tall Girl before she started?"

Small Girl nodded, closed her eyes, took a deep breath in and let it out. Then she opened her eyes and stared into the bird's face. She sat motionless for about an hour.

"Have you got anything?" Teacher asked.

"No. I'm trying but nothing is coming," Small Girl said.

"Time for a break. We've been working for hours with no results, so let's just take some time to relax." Teacher sat back and tipped her head towards the sky.

I looked over at the girls, they both seemed sad and frustrated. I reached over and put my hand on Tall Girl" shoulder.

"It's okay, it doesn't happen overnight, it takes practice."

She nodded, but didn't look any happier. Teacher looked over at the sun which was halfway down the sky. She caught my eye and nodded.

"You try now, Go'diah," she said.

I moved closer to the bird, steadied my breathing and opened myself to him. At first there was nothing, just me looking at the bird. I was starting to feel foolish, but then I felt sad for the poor thing. I looked over at the teacher and let my resentment come to the fore for a moment. She was pushing us too hard. Then I blinked, and without any conscious action on my part I was looking through the bird's eyes. I saw myself, my own face, looking at me, as if I changed places with the bird. It was a bit confusing and I felt disoriented. I glanced at the teacher who was watching me, and in a flash, I was back looking at the bird with my own eyes.

"Huh?" I shook my head to clear it.

"What did you see?" Teacher's voice betrayed her excitement. She looked hard into my face.

"I...I...I'm not sure," I stuttered, as I do when I get put on the spot.

"Did you see something?" she persisted.

I glanced at the other girls. I didn't want to upset them or look like I was trying to make out like I was special or something. I shook my head, no.

Teacher noticed when I glanced at the other girls, and nodded her head. I think she knew I was lying but understood why I did.

"It's time to go, it's getting late," she said. "Small Girl, please pick up the bird and put him in your pocket We're going to keep him safe for the night."

The bird safely in Small Girl's pocket we follow Teacher back to camp. By the time we arrived it was late, and the sun had gone down. Teacher made a fire, brought the remaining rabbit down and spitted it over the fire. Dinner was wonderful, I was so hungry. Small Girl had the bird with her close by, keeping it warm and was watching it for the night. After dinner we decided it was time and said good night to each other and went to bed.

Chapter Four

Day 5
Broken Bones

The day started out well. After we ate, Teacher took the bird out and set it down for us to observe. The poor thing was hardly moving.

"He isn't going to make it to midday unless you three help him," Teacher said raking her gaze over all three of us

She walked over and sat down by the fire. I sat with the other girls by the bird. They seemed as concerned as I was.

"Should we feed try and feed it some worms?" Tall Girl asked.

"If we can find some, it would be worth a try," Small Girl said.

Then they both looked at me.

"Can you help us hunt for some worms?" Tall Girl asked me.

"Sure, I'll help why not?" I got up and stepped carefully away from the tiny bird.

Tall Girl and I walked around looking for dead fall and turning bit over to see what was underneath. We found a few worms and headed back to the camp where Small Girl was watching over the bird. When we came ack to the fire, Small Girl was sitting with the bird, but her eyes were rolled back showing all the white.

"Be quiet," Teachers come over swiftly to stop us saying anything to Small Girl. "She has made a connection with the bird. Let her be."

I was shocked and maybe a bit jealous as Tall Girl and I slowly came closer to observe. Small Girl's head was tipped back, her blank white eyes staring at the sky. She stayed motionless in a trance for what seemed like a long time. Then consciousness came back into her face. She looked up at us and then turned her attention to Teacher.

"The bird is sick with the pain from his wing, and he is hungry as he hasn't been able to hunt for himself.

Tall Girl turned to me with a shocked look on her face which turned to anger when she looked at Small Girl. "How did you do it? How did you connect with the bird and know what he wants?" She pointed at her friend, horror mixed with her anger. "You're a witch!" Tall Girl bolted into the woods in the direction of the falls. Small Girl blinked in confusion and then started to cry.

"It's okay, you're fine. Your friend is upset and probable a bit jealous, but that wasn't a very nice thing she said to you. It's wonderful you managed to connect with the bird, well done. Now if you practice, you can speak to all the animals in time and help them when they need you."

Small Girl smiled and wiped her tears. Tall Girl's scream ripped through the air sending us all jumping to our feet and running toward the falls. We found her by the fishing spot, frozen in place. We skidded to a halt and stared. I almost forgot to breath. A huge bear towered over Tall Girl standing on his hind legs and growling. He must have been seven feet tall and he had her cornered.

Without thinking, just reacting, I ran forward with my hand stretched out toward the bear. Part of me was terrified and wanted to run the other way, but the other part of me was stronger and kept me moving. I slipped into a trance. It was like looking in a mirror. I could see Tall Girl and realized she was afraid of me. I just wanted to tell her it was okay. But I couldn't get the words to come out. Then I heard my voice, but it wasn't my voice. It sounded like a man's voice coming from my throat. *Who is talking?* I thought the question just as the bear's voice echoed in my mind with the same question. Oh my goodness, I'm connected with the bear.

I stilled my heart and quieted my breathing.

"Can I leave now?" the bear's voice was gravelly in my mind.

"Yes, of course. It's okay, we're not here to hurt you you can go whenever you want," I thought the words at him and the echoed in my head.

"I was just hungry and came to go fishing for my lunch when this girl showed up. I stood up to say hello and she scared me when she screamed. Then I screamed," the bear explained.

I laughed. "If you go back down the creek, you can find better fishing. Just walk away and no one well harm you," I told him.

"Okay." The bear dropped to all fours and with a backward glance over his shoulder, walked away.

I flashed back into myself, through my blurred eyes I saw the bear was walking away. Next thing I knew were the sharp rocks I was standing on a moment ago digging into my knees, then just blackness. When I woke up I was back at the camp with the fire was going right beside me. I was in my sleeping bag with a cold rag on my head. I stirred a bit trying to get comfortable. Tall Girl rushed over to me.

"She awake," she called to Teacher.

It was still daylight, I wondered how long I'd been out. The teacher rushed over and knelt beside me.

"How do you feel? Do you remember where you are?" She sounded pretty worried which made me a bit uneasy.

I nodded that I was okay. "I'm thirsty, can I have some water?"

Teacher gave me a cup of water and I drank it all. The water slid down my throat and I could feel it all the way down to my stomach. I handed her back the cup and sat up.

"How long was I out?"

"A few hours," Teacher said. "After establishing a connection that strong with the bear I'm surprised you didn't sleep until tomorrow. It takes a lot of energy to stay open for that length of time."

She turned to question Small Girl as well as me. "What triggered you to connect? One at a time, tell me what allowed you to make that connection."

"For me it was fear. I was scared the bird would die if we couldn't help it," Small Girl said.

'Fear," I said. "I was scared the bear was going to kill one of us, but my courage and love for animals made me overcome the fear and try to tell him to stop. That we weren't a threat to him."

'Interesting." Teacher crossed her arms and walked around the fire. "Fear. That is what triggered both of you, but in different ways. Because you let the love for the bear and animals in general overcome the fear, the courage in your heart allowed you to connect and speak to him in his true voice. Small Girl, in your case it was your willingness to help something smaller and more fragile than yourself that allowed you to connect with the bird."

"Does that mean I need to be scared to make a connection?" Tall Girl asked.

"What happened when you screamed? Were you scared?" Teacher asked.

"Of course I was scared. That was big bear and I was going to die. I saw my life flash before my eyes and everything I wanted to do and wouldn't be able to" Tall Girl's eyes flashed with anger.

"Did you feel the bear?" Teacher asked, ignoring Tall Girl's anger.

"No, I was scared for my life," her voice shook with suppressed anger.

The teacher looked away and changed the subject. "We should get some food," she said and set off into the bush.

I scrambled out of my sleeping bag, grabbed my pack and made myself a cup of coffee and rolled a smoke. The bird was sitting nearby looking around and chirping occasionally. "Have you fed him?" I asked Small Girl.

"Yes, but it's his wing that's hurt and bothering him now."

I looked at the bird and picked him up. Gently, I stretched out his wing to check how much he could move it. The bird chirped and Small Girl rushed over.

"What are you doing? You're hurting him," she protested.

"I'm just checking the wing," I assured her.

Small Girl looked at me like she thought I was planning to eat the little thing. I searched the ground and found a twig big enough to use as support for his wing, I ripped off a small part of my shirt and set the bird on the ground.

"Small Girl, can you help me by holding his wing out so I can get this splint on it and wrap this bit of cloth around it to support the injured part?"

"I guess, but do you know what you're doing? You won't make it worse will you?" Small Girl didn't sound like she trusted me very much.

"I won't hurt him. Hold his wing out and then keep him still until I can get the splint on so it won't fall off," I told her.

Small Girl held the bird still, grimacing in sympathy when the bird complained and tried to get free. Poor guy was in pain, but hopefully the splint would allow the wing to heal and he could fly again. When I was done, Small Girl put the bird down and tried to feed him some worms. He wasn't interested and now he really looked the worse for wear. Getting the splint on took a lot out of him. I felt really bad for the bird.

A while later, Teacher came back with a beaver in her hand. "Does any of you girls know how to clean a beaver?" She dropped the carcass by the fire.

"I do," I said. "I've seen Grandpa do it before and I think I remember what he did." I took the beaver, cleaned it and skinned it. The two girls watched me.

"We've never had to do that, Dad always did the hunting and cleaning," Tall Girl said.

"But we sure know how to cook it," Small Girl said.

They spitted the meat over the fire and before long we were all full. It was late and Teacher got up to check on the bird. He really wasn't looking very well.

"Come, gather round and watch. You must learn how to do this next part," she said. She picked up the bird, went to the falls and came back with some water while we waited by the fire. When she returned she carefully unwrapped the wing, then held the bird in her hand. Her head fell back and her eyes turned white, but only for a second or two. She picked up the water and offered up a prayer. I lit some sage while Teacher blessed the bird and then herself. Murmuring softly, she poured the water over the bird's wing. The wing began to move oddly, making cracking sounds. The bird chirped as if in pain, then slowly he began to move. Soon the wing started to flap, at first slowly, then faster. Suddenly, he was moving both wings, the injured one as well as the other. The wings beat faster, and the bird lifted off her outstretched palm and then flew around Teacher's head, before he flew away.

I gasped in amazement along with the other girls.

"Can you teach us how to do that?" I asked a heartbeat before the other girls asked the same thing.

"First, you must learn to heal yourself, only then can we heal others. Maybe the water will work for you girls too. For now, we need to rest. Tomorrow is another day."

I realized Teacher wasn't going to tell us anything else tonight, I helped pack up the mess from dinner. My thoughts wandered as I worked. So far, two of us had managed to connect with the animals and the earth. Where did that leave Tall Girl?

I crawled into my sleeping bag and looked up into the starry sky where the Dipper watched over us. "Good night, Grandma," I whispered.

Chapter Five

Day 6
Lost vision

Teacher was still asleep when we woke up. That was unusual. Small Girl went over to check on her.

"She's in a deep sleep, I don't' think we should wake her up," she said.

I looked at the sky to gauge the time by the position of the sun. Nine or ten in the morning, I figured. I walked over and moved the girls away from Teacher.

"She needs the rest, she's been teaching us lots and I know from what Grandpa has told me that it takes a lot of energy,". I said.

"Yes, you're right. Let's let her sleep," Tall Girl agreed. "I think I can hunt rabbits and get us some breakfast. I've watched my dad do it."

I wasn't convinced, but my gut said to let her go and try. I looked over at the teacher, she was still sleeping.

"Okay, but don't go too far," I said.

Tall Girl jumped up, clapped her hands and grabbed her pack. She pulled out some snares and headed down the trail. I knew the area a bit, so I wasn't too worried. I was pretty sure I could find her if she got lost as long as she didn't stray too far.

"What can I do to help?" Small Girl asked.

Somehow, they had decided that I was the leader. "Can you go to the falls and catch some fish? But remember about the bear and be sure not to go too far. Be careful."

"I will. I know how to fish now," Small Girl said and disappeared into the forest with the fishing gear.

I started a fire and put on some coffee. Then I pulled out my pack and dug out the Bannock and a bag of dried meat. I turned at a small sound. Teacher was awake. She blinked and sat up quickly. She looked worried and struggled out of her blankets.

"Whoa, slow down," I said holding my hand up palm outward.

"Where the other girls?" she asked.

"We've got this under control. Tall Girl is setting snares for rabbits and Small Girl is fishing. You looked so tired we wanted to let you sleep as long as needed," I told her.

She rolled over and sat up. I poured a cup and gave it to her.

"Thanks," she said, her gaze roaming over the campsite She took a sip of coffee and then motioned for me to come sit beside her. "Go'diah, I need to tell you this. I was lost in my own dreams, and I had to fight to find my way back. I went on a journey of my own and I know I must finish that journey when I have finished teaching you girls."

"I want to go back. Fishing is fun!" Small Girl come into camp with a fish on a string.

"Are you okay now?" I asked Teacher.

"I am," she said, nodding.

"I'll come with you Small Girl. We can catch more fish that way." I stood up and moved to join Small Girl.

"How long has Tall Girl been gone," Teacher asked.

"About forty-five minutes," I said.

Teacher nodded. Small Girl and I set out back to the falls.

We spent about an hour fishing. I caught one fish and just as we were about to pack it in Small Girl caught another one.

"I got another one," she yelled, dancing with excitement. Fish in hand, we headed back to camp.

When we got there, Teacher was standing by the fire with a worried look on her face.

"Tall Girl isn't back yet and it's been almost two hours. Tie those fish up in the tree. We need to go look for her." Teacher waved us toward the tree we'd tied the rabbits up in earlier. It only took a few minutes to secure the fish.

"Which way did she go?" Teacher asked.

Small Girl and I both pointed to the trail Tall Girl had taken. Teacher put her head down and grimaced.

"Ugh, those trails lead everywhere and nowhere. A person could easily get lost if she happened to take the wrong trail." Teacher looked worried.

Small Girl started to panic, grabbing my arm and breathing hard. My heart skipped in my chest.

"I need to meditate. Ask for guidance," Teacher said. She got a hide from her pack, set it down and lowered herself onto it. She took sage, sweetgrass and a feather out of her pack. Then a bowl made of stone.

"Be quiet while I ask for guidance," she told us.

She lit the sage and sweetgrass over the bowl and began to pray.

Small Girl and I sat at a distance and watched her. She prayed for about half an hour, then all of a sudden an eagle flew over the trees near us. It cried loudly as it circled above us in the sky. Teacher opened her eyes; they were white as snow. I knew she was in trance. Her head moved from side to side like the eagle overhead was flying from side to side.

Small Girl stared in amazement at the teacher. Finally, the eagle flew off. I sat and watched the teacher, not knowing what would happen next. The eagle cried again as it returned and landed on a nearby stump.

I looked at Teacher and watched her eyes go from white to grey and back to their normal brown. She blinked a few times, then stood up. "Tall Girl isn't far now and she is safe." Teacher approached the eagle and offered her thanks. The eagle jumped on her shoulder and balanced there. Teacher came over to where Small Girl and I were sitting.

"I want you to meet my friend," she said.

The huge eagle regarded us with his fierce eyes. I returned his gaze, trying hard not to show how scared I was. Small Girl quivered beside me.

Teacher smiled at us.

"I am teaching these two how to control their visions, I could use your help, if you are willing," Teacher addressed the eagle.

The big bird blinked, his head moving from side to side. He gave a chattering cry and flew over to the stump by the fire.

"He has granted us a teaching," Teacher sounded very pleased. She walked over to Small Girl, stood behind her and whispered a word in her ear.

"Repeat it slowly, close your eyes, breathe in and feel the energy around you. Open your heart, your mind to the pure light within you and let it guide you," she instructed her.

Small Girl closed her eyes, let out a deep breath, said the word and opened her eyes. They were white as snow, she had slid into the trance with no problems. The eagle gave a shriek call. I looked over at him, he was moving his wings and looking at itself. Then he looked at us and gave a pealing cry. I looked at Small Girl. She was smiling. She lifted her head and the eagle flew up, circling around us. Small Girl looked down and the eagle came down as well. Small Girl's eyes were back to brown. She grinned and squeaked with excitement. She hugged Teacher.

"I saw through his eyes, and I can fly." Excitement radiated from her.

The teacher laughed. "Wonderful, think you can do it again and this time fly around and see if you can spot Tall Girl?"

"Oh, yes." Small Girl closed her eyes and did it again. This time the eagle flew away over the trees. A few mins later flew back and landed.

Small Girl's eyes are back to normal again. "I saw her, and she looks scared," she reported.

"She'll be fine, I know where she is," Teacher said.

Teacher regarded me thoughtfully. "Think you can do it?"

I met the eagle's gaze and nodded. "I can try."

Teacher moved behind me; her breath ticked my neck as she whispered in my ear.

"We are one. Repeat it slowly, close your eyes, breath in and feel the energy around you. Open your heart, your mind to the pure light within you and let it guide you." The air moved slightly as she stepped away.

I closed my eyes and relaxed. My body filled with warmth and I almost thought I might float off the ground. I took a deep breath and let it out. "We are one. We are one. We are one."

Bright light flashed against my closed eyelids. Startled I opened my eyes. I was the eagle. I could see the three people staring at me: Small Girl, Teacher and me with my head thrown back, white eyes turned to the sky. I couldn't believe how strong the connection was. My vision was amazing. I could see almost 360 degrees around me. I admired the span of my wings spread out on either side of me. I made a conscious effort to move those wings and incredibly they responded to my thoughts. I took some deeper strokes with my wings and picked up speed, flapping harder and faster. Then suddenly I was lifting off the stump. I was actually flying, while my corporeal body stood far below where I soared. The experience was more than I ever could have imagined. The wind was strong beneath my wings, I was aware of every feather and how it responded to the moving air. I could see the whole mountain. I flew toward the trees, taking in every detail with my magnified sight. As I coasted further over the forest on the air currents I saw Tall Girl. I estimated she was about 15 or 20 minutes away from the camp. But she looked lost and was heading in the wrong direction. Spinning around on a wingtip, I glided back to the campsite to let Teacher know. I settled on the stump, my talons digging into the soft wood. It was odd looking out of the eagle's eyes and seeing myself standing in front of me. I shifted uneasily on the stump trying to return to my body. A huge wave of dizziness swept over me making me want to throw up. I was stuck! I couldn't shake myself loose from the eagle. I opened my mouth and startled myself when the scream of an eagle came from my throat. Teacher moved in front of me, commanding me to look at her just by her physical and mental presence.

"Go'diah! Go'diah! Look at me. Feel the earth, feel your physical body. Come back!" Teacher clapped her hands in front of my face. The sound of the sharp crack broke my connection and I fell to my knees in my own body.

The eagle flew away and I got to my feet, swaying slightly and rubbing my hands across my face.

"What happened? What made you panic like that?" Teacher looked concerned.

"I was stuck. I couldn't break the connection and then I got really dizzy and sick feeling," I said. I kept my head down. Maybe I did something wrong or something I shouldn't have...

"What brought you back?"

"You did. Your voice and when you clapped your hands," I said.

Teacher dropped her gaze and sighed. "You need something you are connected strongly to in order to keep part of you grounded in your own mind. You can't give yourself over totally to whatever creature you have connected with. Next time, think of your Grandpa being here guarding you and holding space while you travel. You will be able to return safely."

"Okay, that's what I'll do," I said, raising my head and letting out a breath of relief. I didn't do anything wrong. Thank goodness.

"Did you see Tall Girl in your flight?" Teacher asked.

"Yes, I did. But she was going in the wrong direction"

"Which way did she go? Teacher looked over my shoulder at the forest.

"Up the side of the mountain," I said.

Teacher moved quickly to her pack, grabbed her knife and slid it into the sheath on her back. "Don't go anywhere," she yelled before she ran into the forest.

I sat down and checked the position of the sun in the sky. It was just above the tree line, so maybe four in the afternoon. Small Girl threw more wood on the fire and stood staring into the flames. I decided to clean the fish and went to take them down from the tree. Small Girl came to help me.

"What do you think of all this stuff?" Small Girl asked me while we were cleaning the fish.

I looked up and shrugged my shoulders. "It's cool!! I like it."

She smiled "Me too. Maybe if I get good enough I can bring the dead back to life." She grinned in a weird way and picked up her fish to go and wash the blood off of it.

Something in my stomach twisted at her word. What she just said really wasn't good at all. Not in any way.

Teacher and Tall Girl emerged from the woods laughing. Tall Girl caught three rabbits.

"I almost got lost, good thing you cam looking for me." Tall Girl laughed and put the rabbits by the fire.

I caught Teacher's eye and managed to let her know I needed to talk to her in private. She nodded to let me know she understood. That evening after dinner she asked us to get our gowns out.

"The moon is just right to teach us to dance," she said.

I was excited and the other two girls seemed to be too. I wondered what dancing with the moon was all about. All three of us got into our gowns and stood by the fire to keep warm. Teacher came out of the bush with four long pieces of willow with the buds on them. She showed us how to make a head band and we put them on our heads. Then she told us a story of the old ways and how they use to dance under the full mood to give thanks for another year and asked to be blessed in the coming years with our gifts as healers.

The teacher built up the fire, got it nice and big. Next, she took some herbs & flowers out of her pack. When she laid each one down, she told us the meaning behind that plant. Baby's breath flowers for love, bay leaves for positive energy, white orchid for peace, and sage for protection. She laid them all down on a hide where they would be easy to grab. Then she pulled a small drum from her pack. I kept notes and rhythms in my head and paid close attention. I was eager to learn and was enthralled with all the new things I was being taught.

She started by singing and hitting the drum, it was beautiful. I had heard my grandparents sing before, but nothing like this. She sang so softly, peacefully, and the melody was one I never heard before. It had a nice beat that seemed to call to me. She got up and started to dance and sing. I got to my feet and joined her, the other girls followed me. It was a happy tune that rose with the smoke of the campfire. Teacher grabbed a hand full of flowers and herbs and looked at us.

"Each of you take an offering," she said through her singing.

I picked up a handful of the fragrant flowers and herbs, the scent sweet in my nose. I danced with the others following the beat of the drum. Joy filled my heart with each beat and note of the song. The moon's energy shone down on me, the warmth of the earth flowed upward through me.

"Can you feel the energy?" Teacher asked.

"Yes, oh yes," I said in unison with the others.

Teacher threw her bundle of flowers and herbs in the fire. I fed mine to the flames as well.

"Thank you, Creator for all our blessings, and thank you for another year," Teacher yelled once all the bundles were tossed into the fire. Then she took off her head band and tossed it in the fire as well. We followed her lead. Laughs with joy, she sat on the ground, catching her breath. "Wow, it's been a year already. And this year, I have had the honor of dancing with the next healers and teachers."

We all smiled at her and at each other, the moment was one I would never forget.

The teacher smiled and looked at the moon. "I remember when I first had my teacher, I was no older then you three. I will always remember what she said," Teacher paused and looked at each of us, "our awakening is not about who we are, but of who and what we become. True power comes to us under the full moon when the rhythm of nature becomes one with our souls. But do not underestimate the energy, anything unresolved in your realm, will manifest itself and eat away at your energy realm until it is healed. Pay close attention. Never let negative energy in and always let the light guide you."

She stood up. "Time for bed now, tomorrow is another day."

The girls and I changed into something warmer and crawled in our sleeping bags. What a day. I said my prayers and went to sleep.

Chapter Six

Day 7
Water Healing

The day began early. I blinked and shivered in the cold when I crawled out of my sleeping bag.

"It's day seven of your teachings, and today we will only be doing one lesson and some meditation for our spirit guide to come to us, to show us who will guide us from this point on."

I was excited to meet my spirit guide. We prepared for the hike by filling our water sacks made from moose bellies that Teacher had gifted us with. We hiked into the forest where Teacher connected with a hurt animal.

"Can you find the connection with the injured animal?" Teacher asked us. All three of us drop into a trance. I find the creature, as does Small Girl, but Tall Girl is still struggling. Still in our trance, Small Girl and I follow the connection to a fox. He was trapped, both legs were broken and pinned with rocks. He was crying for help but there was no one around except us.

"Who has the connection?" Teacher asked

Small Girl and I answer together, "I do."

"Do you know where he is?" Teacher asked.

I looked through the fox's eyes. "In the trees somewhere nearby?"

"Are there birds nearby?" Teacher coached us.

"Yes," I said.

"Then look through the bird and see if you can find a landmark to guide you," Teacher said.

It was hard to jump from one animal to the other. Small Girl lost her connection, but I held on to mine. I focused on the bird. It was as if my eyes blinked and then I was looking through the bird's eyes. Sending a thought supported by energy I asked the bird to lead us to the fox. The bird came nearer and found us. In the bird, I swooped down and flew around the teacher. She nodded and the group followed the bird. The fox was near, not too far off, just over a hill. Teacher found the fox and waved to the bird. I snapped back, got to my feet and followed them to where the fox was.

Small Girl and Teacher moved the rocks away from the fox. He couldn't move and was whining a lot in pain. Teacher connected with the fox and calmed him. While still in a trance she yelled for us to move the fox to flat ground while she has him safe in the connection. The girls and I moved quick, putting our hands under him so we could we move him to the flat part of ground covered in the leaves. Tears ran down Teacher's face as she took the fox's pain into herself to ease him. She released the connection and sat down. The fox passed out from the pain.

Panic is sweeping over me and I see the other two girls aren't in any better shape.

"Calm down! This is all part of our teaching today," Teacher shouted at us.

I control my emotions and watch to see what she does. Teacher leaned over the fox and held his leg. She looked at both legs deciding what needed to be done.

"Small Girl and Tall Girl, each of you take one side. I will guide you through what bones are injured how to heal them with the water Mother Nature has provided," Teacher instructed.

The girls move one on each side.

"Each of you hold the broken leg on your side," Teacher's voice is calm.

"It's shattered. I can't even hold it up," Tall Girl exclaimed.

"Trust in yourself, close your eyes and feel the energy running through the earth. Now let that energy pass through you and through your hands. Feel the fox's energy and see the bones in the light of that energy. Once you have that clearly in sight, take your water and ask Creator to heal the energy that is broken. Pour the water when you can feel the life energy through the water," Teacher instructed them.

It was silent while I watched them. I closed my eyes and breathed. I saw the energy and heard the pulse of the earth's heart in every strand of energy. It was loud and clear in my mind. I felt the fox's legs, both of them. From where I was sitting I could see the bones, felt the heartbeats of everyone around me. It was like we were all connected, part of the whole. In unison, both girls got their water out, and asked the Creator to help them heal the fox. I opened my eyes. They poured their water and the fox woke, screaming in pain. Nothing had happened, it didn't' work. The girls couldn't do it.

My mouth fell open I shock. I thought Small Girl for sure had managed it.

"Let us try again," Small Girl pleaded.

"One more try," Tall Girl insisted.

"One more, that is all," Teacher said.

I felt sorry for the poor fox. Teacher walked them through it one more time, but the result was the same. The poot fox woke up keening in pain.

Teacher put a hand on his head and puts him to sleep. "Poor baby." Her gaze rakes over us.

The two girls are upset and Small Girl started to cry. Her face got red with anger and she looked away from Teacher and the fox. Tall Girl, didn't seem to care too much.

Teacher looked over at me. "Care to try?" She sounded discouraged and disappointed.

'Teacher's pet," Small Girl snarled at me.

Teacher looked at her and then swept all of us with her gaze. "*No one* is a pet to this teacher." Frustration roughened her voice. "You can't learn this stuff in one try, unless you have accepted your bloodline's calling. A child born of the healer's bloodline has a chance to be born with the gift of healing. That is through no fault or choice of their own. They must accept the gift or move on. Some have it in them, and some just don't. Those who don't, still learn and tell the true stories."

Both girls looked embarrassed and didn't meet my eye. I joined Teacher by the fox.

"Did you hear the instructions I gave the other girls?" she asked me.

"I did," I said.

"Then go ahead, see if you can heal him."

I put my hand on one of his legs and I closed my eyes. I could see the shattered bones. I allowed the energy to flow through me began with the big part of the bone. It was like putting a puzzle together. In no time, I could see the bone start to look whole again. Once the first leg seemed to be in line, I worked on the other leg. It wasn't as hard as the first one since I'd had some practice. I took the water and poured it over both legs. I could see the water's energy and everything healing together.

"Thank you," I whispered the Creator and the energy.

Shortly afterward, the fox woke up and blinked. Carefully, it moved both its legs then jumped up and licked us all. With a happy bark it ran off into the woods.

"Thank you, thank you," his little fox voice rang in my mind.

"You're welcome," I sent back to him before the connection faded.

I looked at the teacher. "You're a great teacher," I sent to her with my mind.

"Thank you, good job," she replied in my head.

This was so great, to be able to talk without words being said out loud. I could share things like this that I couldn't if I'd spoken them out loud. I told her about my concerns with Small Girl. Teacher replied that she had senses something dark in the girl but wasn't ready to act yet.

"Can we go and eat?" Tall Girl asked, breaking the connection between Teacher and myself.

"Of course, let's go," Teacher agreed.

While we were eating, Tall Girl and Small Girl both wanted to know why they hadn't been able to heal the fox. Teacher did her best to answer them. I kept quiet and just listened. After dinner Teacher told us a story and then we all went to bed.

Chapter Seven

Day 8
Rest & Meditation

Another early start to the day. Teacher made a great breakfast and then we went to the falls. She sets us up by the falls, each of us with a hide to sit on. We all picked our own spots that we felt most connected too. Everyone was all over the area, but we were close enough for help if anything happened. We were all comfy and settled down to begin the lesson. I could hear the birds, the water, the breeze, the trees, the bushes, the squirrels running through the trees. Somewhere far off I could hear frogs. I could hear everything around me. It was like I was dreaming, I could see the energy like strips of lights that flew through everything real fast. It was beautiful. In this level of meditation we can hear each other's thoughts. Small Girl told me a joke and I giggled out loud. Everything was at a distance. I opened my eyes and looked down. Small Girl was looking back at me and laughing with her hand over her mouth. I giggled. Crazy girl, I thought. I slipped back into meditation and connected with all the animals around me.

I saw, bears, wolves, rabbits, foxes, mountain lions, moose, caribou, buffalo, martins, beavers, all kinds of wood land creatures. They were coming at me from all sides, then passing through me. One by one they came, it was just beautiful. Then one animal came and I waited for it pass through like al the others had so far. This time, the animal stood in front of me and stared into my face. It was a female mountain bear. She walked around me and sat behind me. I could feel her energy on my back like a light. We merged as one. I opened my eyes and I felt the strength of the bear in me. I was different, wiser, bigger...I am fierce, fearless, and something woke in me. I looked around and could see everything so clearly now. I got up and went over to the teacher.

"I need rest at the fire," I said, feeling a bit exhausted but energized at the same time.

"Your spirit guide has shown itself to you and claimed you. I can see by the white streak of wisdom in your hair. Which animal was it?" Teacher asked.

"Bear. I feel weak. I need to rest," I said, feeling myself start to slip in and out of consciousness.

Teacher supported me and I leaned on her as she took me to my sleeping bag and put me down on it. She gave me a sip of water and I drank. My vision darkened and I slipped into the dark. I woke up to find the teacher with the girls eating dinner and talking about me. I moved my arm and tried to sit up.

"Are you okay?" Tall Girl rushed to me.

I blinked. "yes, I must have passed out."

Tall Girl picked up a strand of my hair in her hand and looked at it. I looked too and realized it was white. *What the heck?* I scrambled up.

"Am I old now?" My voice rose to a squeaky pitch.

They all laughed at me.

"Why would you ask that?" Teacher said.

I held out a piece of my hair. "Well, maybe this white hair I have is making me ask."

More laughter, which I didn't think was funny at all.

"Calm down, I'll explain it all after you are properly awake and have some food in your belly," Teacher tells me.

I nodded and sat by the fire while Tall Girl got me a plate of food and a drink. I looked over at Small Girl to find her glaring at me. I could feel her anger. I decided to read her thoughts. They came through loud and clear: *I wish you just died.* I dropped my bowl, and she looked away. I didn't know what to say but needed to explain why I dropped my dinner.

"Must have just been the shakes," I said.

"Something I should know, girls?" Teacher asked, her gaze boring into me.

Small Girl glared at me and I heard her thoughts again: *Go ahead and snitch. Pet.* Her expression was venomous.

I refused to back down: *I can hear every word you think, so don't push it.*

A ripple of shock ran over her face, followed by anger and fear. She stood up and pointed at me. "She's making fun of me and listening to my thoughts," Small Girl accused me.

Teacher stood up. "Go sit down. Now. And if you ever yell at me again, I well make you walk home alone," she threatened Small Girl.

Small Girl was furious, she strode off towards the falls. Teacher looked at me and raised an eyebrow.

"Can you explain to me what just happened there?"

I shook my head. "Forget it."

"You must find peace in these energy realms we sleep in," she told me.

I nodded in agreement. I sat up and finished eating. Before long Small Girl came back and sat at the fire.

"I'm sorry, I just got jealous when you started experiencing more than me. I was just foolish I guess," Small Girl said. Then she got up and went to her sleeping bag and crawled in, turning her back to me.

"You need to join us, Small Girl. I have a story to share with you," Teacher said.

Grumbling under her breath, Small Girl came back to the fire.

The teacher got the fire hot and looked at the stars. She told us a story about how over a hundred years ago healers were all over and practiced medicine openly. But then one by one the healers disappeared and were lost with time.

"Our journey for the next two days will be returning to the village," she paused, looked up again and continued, "there is a test that must happen when we return. The spirits have spoken to me, and the time has come for the medicine man to prove that he is worthy of keeping his title as the village healer." She sighed. "He has not been able to understand the dreams that have haunted the village for far too many moons, and you," pointed her finger at me, "at such a young age, took a journey to the mountains to get answers. To find the truth, meet with the spirits, and pass all the tests of the healers in just days. Your bloodline is of the first bloodline, it is strong within you. It was the visions that brought Go'diah to my dreams. To make the wrong right again and to set the balance back to align the mountain's energy."

She continued to talk about her vision and how she knew to find us. "I saw your village through the fog. The medicine man's house, we saw one another, he knew of me. A women appeared to us and warned him, she sent me to teach and prepare three girls for a test, to hold the true bloodline to the rightful name of healer. I saw three houses and three girls. Only one shall prove their true self, and that was all I saw," Teacher said. She sat back with a sigh and the silence settled over the campsite.

I looked at the fire in silence trying to take it all in. Wow, I was lost for words.

"So, you're telling us that when we get home we have to pass some kind of test? And it's with the man who is the healer now?" Tall Girl demanded. She swallowed hard. "That old man is scary, and I'm too scared to try, I don't want to do it." She sat down.

"I can do it, I can take him on," Small Girl boasted.

"The test has already been given to me to lay out, and we shall decide how to proceed back at the village, now we must sleep," Teacher said.

We all went to bed around the fire. I lay there thinking about how much I just missed my grandma and grandpa. All I wanted to do was hold them and ask my grandpa to make me his famous moose stew, I was feeling home sick and willed myself to fall asleep.

Chapter Eight

Day 9
Changing of the Clouds

Day nine was a lazy one. I rolled out of my sleeping bag later than usual. The other girls were just getting up as well. Teacher was up and ready to go, she must have been sitting and watching us sleep. I wandered over to the fire and had something to eat. I looked at the sun and figured it was about nine in the morning. Teacher was right you could tell time just by looking at the sun, and I'd learned how to do that.

"Today before we leave, please put everything down and let's learn this last lesson," Teacher said.

I put my pack down beside the other two.

"Feel the sky and the energy around the clouds. Focus on the clouds: feel them as if they were cotton and you can move them around. Feel the wind up in the sky and move the energy around," Teacher instructed us while she demonstrated what she wanted us to try.

It looked so cool and when I tried to copy her, it wasn't so hard. All three of us girls had fun playing with the clouds for a while. It was really easy once I got the hang of using the energy borrowed from the wind. There was so much I wanted to tell my grandma when I got home.

The air vibrated with excitement while we packed and got ready to leave the campsite. I stopped at the edge of the clearing and looked back. "I will be back," I promised, just as I had the last time I left my camp on the mountain. We followed Teacher down the trail. To my annoyance Teacher began pulling down the orange flags I left earlier on my first journey.

"Hey, that's my markers. I left them so I could find my way back. Leave them alone," I said, panting a bit from running to catch up with her.

Teacher stopped and looked at me. Her expression wavered between disgust and disappointment. She held my gaze as if waiting for me to figure out what I'd done wrong. It dawned on me like a bolt of light. I didn't need the markers, I had vision now, I could find the trail now without the markers. I shook my head wordlessly. She smiled and shook her head when she was sure I'd figured it out.

We continued down the trail until we got to the first camp site. The hike took us 7 hours and I tired. Without much talking we set up the camp, made a quite meal and then everyone crawled into their sleeping bags.

__Day 10__
__Home at Last__

I woke up eager to get on the trail. We were almost home. Teacher hurried us through breakfast. I wasn't sure why she was in such a hurry, but I wasn't complaining. I had so much to tell Grandpa and Grandma, and I missed Midnight. Teacher set a fast pace and arrived back at our village around a quarter to six in the evening. Small Girl and Tall Girl split off in different directions and hurried toward their homes. Teacher went over to the medicine man's house and disappeared inside. I ran the last few feet to our home. I opened the door and surprised them.

Grandpa and Grandma are sitting at the table with Uncle. They jumped to their feet shouting their greetings and hugging me. Grandma fussed over me like I was a baby. Grandpa went to the stove and made me some coffee while Uncle rolled me a smoke. It was so nice to be home. I took a deep breath and let out a sigh of relief. Grandma noticed my hair right away and she showed me her white streak of wisdom. The white was blended in with the hair that had turned grey with age. I loved her so much and told her so. Grandpa unpacked my pack, and Grandma made me something to eat. Nobody would let me do anything but sit at the table and relax.

"Tell us about your journey," Uncle asked me, leaning his elbows on the table.

"Yes, tell us everything," Grandpa said.

"I can only tell a bit of it tonight. I've been sleeping on the ground for ten days and hiking all over the mountain. I'm so tired I could fall asleep sitting here."

I did manage to share a bit of what happened on the mountain, but Grandma could tell I just wanted to go crawl in my bed.

"Tomorrow, Go'diah can tell us more tomorrow." Grandma led me into my bedroom and tucked me into bed. I fell asleep almost before I had closed my eyes.

Chapter Nine

Day 1
First day of the Test
    Grandpa was cooking bacon, the smell drifted through the whole house and woke me up. I could hear Grandma talking to Uncle. I smiled and stretched out the aches in my body. *Oh my God, I'm in my bed and it's heaven.* I had the best sleep I'd had in days. I got up and got dressed. When I left my room Uncle was having a coffee at the table. Grandma was in the living room watching a small black and white tv and listening to the news. Grandpa poured me a coffee. "Come, sit, have some coffee and eat. You have a big day you need to be ready for."

    I glanced at the clock. Nine a.m. Wow, I really slept in. It was nice of them not to wake me up. I was just finished eating when someone knocked on the door. Grandpa opened it and Teacher was standing there. Grandpa invited her in and she greeted my family. She sat at the table and accepted a coffee from Grandma. Teacher began to tell my family about the journey, and her story took some time to tell. I couldn't believe she remembered every little detail. When she was finished, she set her coffee down.

"Your granddaughter is the most strongest young healer I have seen in my life time. I witnessed things in the mountains that the old stories speak of. I'm very proud of Go'diah. You have done a good job or raising her." Teacher shook Grandpa's hand. "Which side of the bloodline is the ability to heal through?"

"It is mine," Grandma said.

"It is an honor to teach your granddaughter." Teacher got to her feet and turned to leave. She stopped and look right at me. "Be ready. The first test is at noon when the sun is high."

I nodded. I had no idea what the test was going to be, but I knew I could handle it.

Grandma hugged me. "I am the proudest grandma alive today," she laughed, "I'm just going to walk downtown with my new shoes and gloves and brag." Laughter broke out in the kitchen and we spent a few minutes joking and enjoying each other's company. Before I realized how much time had passed Teacher knocked on the door.

"Are you ready?" she asked when I opened the door.

I looked at Grandpa and Grandma and swallowed hard. They rushed and got their coats on with Uncle right behind them. It was the most excitement our family had in a long time. When everyone was ready, we gathered at the hall in the village where everyone else was waiting for us. The teacher stepped forward and started to talk about our journey in the mountains with her. I stood with the other two girls behind her while she spoke. Tall Girl preened like she'd just won a princess pageant. Small Girl stood beside her trying to look as tall as possible and like she expected something special was about to happen to her. Neither of them looked at me when I joined them. Small Girl's parents were glaring at everyone. I just ignored them and listened carefully. Teacher was explaining about the upcoming three tests for that day and how the three girls would compete with Joe, the current medicine man.

"The first test will be The Gift of Healing," she announced. She looked at each of us in turn. "As the current medicine man, Joe, you will go first."

Joe stepped forward and someone guided in a man that had a broken finger. He had smashed it while chopping tree stumps in his back yard. The medicine man approached him and brought out his water bag. He began his the healing ritual as the teacher lit sage in little pots at all four points of the room.

Joe seemed to be struggling, sweat poured down his brows and his head band was soaked. I bit my lip in sympathy while I watched. The injured man screamed for a few minutes and fell to the floor. The medicine man collapsed next to him, drained of energy. A hush fell over the hall and Teacher rushed to his side to check his heart rate. She helped him up to sit in a chair. Joe waved his arm to indicate the healing was complete. The man on the floor got up and showed everyone that his hand was healed. Everyone clapped.

Up next was Tall Girl. She stepped forward and stopped. "I am truly sorry, but this is one test I cannot do. I failed this one on our journey," she confessed with her head down. Her dad come and hugged her.

"It's okay, girl. It takes courage to admit when we can't do something," Teacher tells her, patting her on shoulder.

"Next," Teacher yelled and pointed at me.

I stepped forward and took a deep breath. *I can do this.* I looked at Grandpa and he nodded at me. An old man was brought in. He had broken his arm while falling on a pile of wood. I smiled nervously at him and approached him. I put both my hands on him, one top of the break and one under his arm. I had my bag by my side, comforting weight on my hip. I breathed in and let out all the doubt, fear, and negativity. I opened myself and concentrated. The energy answered to my call, starting as a sprinkle of little lights, then sparks of energy started to flow faster. I could see everything and the energy of everyone around me. I see the old man's arm with my inner vision. His bones are so frail and I knew I had to work carefully. I began to put the bone together like a puzzle as gently as I could manage. The old man screamed, and I targeted the part of his brain that felt pain and numbed it, took some of the pain into myself as I'd seen Teacher do with the fox. The old man stopped screaming and I kept working on him, sweat trickling down my spine. A few moments later, I poured the water from my bag and heard a breath of relief escape his lips. The bruises faded and he could move his arm as though it had never been injured. He got up and hugged me. My head was a little fuzzy and my vision blurred at bit when I looked up. But my energy was still strong. The applause shook the rafters of the hall. I looked over at my grandma and she was smiling so hard she had a tear rolling down her face. I smiled and waved at her before I sat in the chair that was provided and took a drink of water. Joe nodded at me in approval.

"Small Girl is next," Teacher announced beckoning her forward. She walked to the front, and everyone had their eyes on her. An old woman with a broken leg was brought in. She had tripped over a log and broke the leg a week ago. The injured woman was helped into a chair where everyone could see. Small Girl walked over with her water bag hanging on her belt. The crowd was silent as she started her healing ritual. Small Girl pulled up another chair and sat holding the woman's leg with her eyes closed and an expression of fierce concentration on her face. Teacher waited forty-five minutes before she approached them.

Small Girl, stop this now," Teacher said.

"I got this," Small Girl screamed in frustration. "Leave me alone, it will just take a bit longer. I got this!"

Teacher looked into Small Girl's face and took a step back in shock. "Stop! Stop right now," Teacher yelled.

I craned my neck to see what had upset the teacher so much. Small Girl's eyes were open a slit and they were pure black, not the white of healing. *Oh my God!*

Small Girl snarled and took her hands away from the old woman's leg. She got up and went back to the chair beside Tall Girl. She didn't say another word. Teacher approached the old woman and healed her leg. The old woman got up and walked around to show the leg was healed. There was subdued clapping. Small Girl's parents didn't look happy at all.

"The second test will be The Gift of Vision," Teacher announced.

A boy from the village volunteered to go hide in the woods and wait for us to find him. The boy left the hall and ran off into the forest. We were required to wait for an hour and prepare ourselves before we could begin.

"The time is up now, the healers must come forward and find the missing boy," Teacher addressed the crowd. "Up first is Joe, the medicine man."

Joe came forward and sat on the floor. I thought he looked pretty weak, but I knew better than to underestimate him. He said he was planning to use the eyes of the Raven as Raven has such sharp vision. He fell into a trance to begin his vision quest ,and his eyes turned white. He moved his head, then without more than a few minutes passing he snaped back and fell forward on his hand. Teacher went to assist him but he waved her away.

"I'm fine and the boy is found," Joe said.

"You, please go and check where the boy is hidden then come back and tell us the location," Teacher asked one of the young men in the crowd. Then she turned to Joe. "Tell us where you found the boy."

Joe described the hollow tree he had found the boy hiding near. Then we waited for the two boys to return. It took about twenty minutes before they entered the hall.

"Where did you hide?" Teacher asked the young boy.

"A little way into the forest I hid behind a big hollow tree that I knew was there," he said.

Everyone clapped and Joe smiled.

"Tall Girl, you're next," Teacher said.

Tall Girl came forward and folded her hands in front of her. "I pass, I don't want to do this," she said and returned to her chair.

I nodded at her and whispered, "It's okay." She gave me a tiny smile in return.

"Go'diah, you are next," Teacher called me to the front. She sent the boy off to find another hiding place and I waited for her to give me the signal to begin.

I hadn't thought of which animal it would be best to use. I sat down on the floor, crossed my legs and let my hands rest on my knees. "I will be using the eagle, for he is a hunter with sharp eyes," I announced. I let myself fall into a trance. It only took me a few seconds to find an eagle and then search for the boy. The eagle seemed to know what I needed as he went directly to where the boy was hiding without hardly any guidance from me. I snapped back. "I found him," I announced. I grinned up at Teacher.

She sent another boy to get the one who was hiding. While they were gone she questioned me. "Where was he hiding?"

"There is a tall tree that the boys like to climb. He was sitting in the crotch of the big maple tree that is next to the river crossing," I said.

Thirty minutes later the two boys returned. "Where were you hiding?" Teacher asked the boy.

"I climbed that big old maple tree by the river crossing. Hardly anyone every looks up when they are looking for someone," he announced with a cheeky grin.

Everyone clapped and I went back to my chair.

"Small Girl, you're next," Teacher said. She sent another boy out to hide in the forest and we waited until she gave Small Girl the signal to begin.

Small Girl came forward and sank down onto the floor. "I'm going to use a small bird," she said. Her head fell back and in a matter of minutes she opened her eyes. "I have found him."

Teacher sent someone out to bring back the third boy. "Where did you find the boy," she asked Small Girl.

"It was easy," she said in a smug tone, "he hid that old woodshed just inside the trees."

It didn't take long for the two boys to come back. "Where were you hiding?" Teacher asked the third boy.

He shrugged. "I didn't go far. I just hid in that old woodshed. You know the one just inside the tree," he said.

Everyone clapped and Small Girl returned to her chair, giving me a challenging look as she passed me.

"The third test is The Gift of Medicine," Teacher announced. "Joe, you're first."

Joe went to the table Teacher had set up in front of the crowd. He brought all his herbs with him and started to mix and boil over the small brazier in the middle of the table. I watched and shook my head with surprise. I didn't think you should mix those particular leaves together, but I kept quiet and waited to see what he had planned. A young boy in the village had the stomach flu and needed medicine. The boy was brought up to Joe who prepared the medicine and handed it to the boy's mother.. He instructed her to make him drink it. The boy drank the medicine and immediately started to cry in pain. A gasp rippled through the crowd. The child dropped to the ground and rolled around in pain. Panic contorted Joe's face and he scrambled to prepare another mixture. He shoves it into the mother's hand and tells her to make the boy take it. She gets it down her son's throat but all it did was make the boy puke. Finally, he stopped vomiting and seemed to be feeling better. Joe looked really relieved when everyone clapped as the boy quit crying. Joe returned to his chair, glancing at Teacher who didn't look very impressed.

"Go'diah is next," Teacher said pointing at me.

I got to my feet and suddenly realized that Tall Girl had slipped away while I was watching Joe and the sick boy. Even her chair was gone. I took a breath. *Okay, so it's only the three of us now.* I moved to the table which was now cleared of Joe's things and set my own ingredients in place. I waited for the teacher to send me the person I was to heal. A woman came forward with a little boy.

"What is his complaint," I asked the mother.

"His poor little tummy is very upset and he can't keep anything in his stomach," she told me.

I put the little one on the edge of the table and ran my hands over his tummy. I smiled at him in a reassuring way before handing him back to his mom. I made up a batch of basil tea and after it cooled, I fed it to him with a spoon. Before long, he was smiling and his stomach was feeling much better.

"Thank you," his mother said as they returned to their seats in the crowd

Everyone clapped as I sat down.

"Small Girl, you are up now," Teacher called her to the front.

She was presented with a person with a rash on their arm. Without speaking to the person at all, Small Girl made an ointment and slathered it on the woman. The woman squeaked in pain for a moment and then smiled as the pain and itchiness went away.

"Well done," Teacher said to Small Girl.

"That concludes the testing for today," Teacher told the crowd. "Round Two is tomorrow. I strongly suggest the three people being tested get some rest."

I was happy the testing was over for the day and I joined my family for the walk home. It had been a long day and I was tired even though it was only seven in the evening.

"You did well, Sprout," Grandpa said and hugged me

"Guess I shouldn't tease you anymore," Uncle teased me.

Our laughter drifted through the air as we climbed the steps to our door. Grandpa made dinner for us to give Grandma a bit of a break. Then I went to bed.

Chapter Ten

Day 2
Second day of the Test

Everyone was up early again, I hadn't slept well, but I felt ready to meet whatever challenge Teacher had in store for me. The sky looked a little cloudy, I wondered if it was going to rain. Maybe if it rained they would hold off on today's test. A knock sounded on the door. Uncle opened it and invited Teacher inside. She stopped just at the door.

"I have come to inform you that Small Girl will not be in today's test," Teacher said.

"Why?" I couldn't help asking.

"She can't fight for the title of medicine woman if she can't heal a broken bone," Teacher said.

I was pretty sure there was more to it than what she was saying. Teacher sat at the table and the thought occurred to me that could read her thoughts. I knew I shouldn't, but my curiosity won over my commonsense. I tried to slip into her mind but within seconds blew me out of her head and towered over me in a rage. "Never do that to me or anyone else ever again," she hurled the words at me and stalked out.

"What did you do?" Grandpa yelled at me.

I looked down in shame and ran to my room. I screwed up really badly. I laid on my bed and cried a bit. But it was my own fault, I shouldn't have tried to do that. I reached out to her from my room and found her connection. *Sorry.* I sent the thought full of contrition. Teacher answered me. *I'm sorry too.* I opened my eyes and broke the connection. I stayed in my room until Grandpa knocked on my door to tell me it was time for the test. "Let's go," he said.

We went to the hall where everyone was gathered already. It was just me and the medicine man.

"Small Girl will no longer be part of the testing." Teacher waited for the rumbled of voices settled again. "The next test is the Gift of Cloud Changing," she announced. "Joe, you are first."

The medicine man stepped outside the hall and everyone followed behind Teacher and me. Joe walked to the center of the road where he waved his staff around and around. All our eyes were on the sky. There was nothing happening that I could see. He tried again and again. Finally, he lowered his arms and walked toward the people gathered in the road. "When was the last time I had to stop the sun from shining?" Joe joked, although his eyes weren't laughing with everyone else. "It's been too long, and I can't remember how to do this anymore."

"It's okay, don't' worry about it." Teacher tapped Joe on the back in a friendly gesture. She came to where I was standing by the hall door. "It's your turn, Go'diah," she said.

I took a deep breath and let it out slowly to calm my heart, then moved to the center of the road. I closed my eyes and raised my arms, connecting with the clouds overhead. I remembered how much fun it was when I was learning how to move them. The clouds danced and moved in time with my arms. *I did it!* I opened my eyes when everyone clapped. Teacher nodded at me with a secret smile.

"There is only one final test to be faced," Teacher told the gathered villagers. "Since two of the original four candidates have not qualified to move on, this test will be short. The final test is between the last two, Joe and Go'diah. Their spirit guides will do battle. Whichever spirit animal is the strongest will win for the person they are connected with the title of medicine man or woman for this generation in this village. The test begins now." Teacher stepped back.

Joe whipped off his shirt before I realized what was happening. I blinked. A huge black wolf sprang out of his chest. The crowd gasped and some screamed. The black wolf snarled at the people nearest him, growled and leaped back into Joe's chest.

Oh my God! That dream I had on my first night of the journey...a huge black wolf attacked my face. My dream was warning me. I knew it was him. Wow, I thought, Joe knew about my quest even before I even did. He must have sensed I was looking for the medicine hidden inside me.

A smattering of applause rippled through the crowd. Teacher signaled for me to begin as Joe stepped back.

I knelt on the ground, connecting with the earth and the heavens. I looked up, took a deep breath, and closed my eyes. Immediately, I could feel my guide coming. When she manifested, she came hard. A huge bear stood on her hind legs in front of me. She opened her mouth, and a massive growl issued from her throat, shaking the whole building. Then she dropped to all fours and slid back into me. I was honored and in awe. The Great Mother Bear was my spirit guide and she accepted me in front of my village. The protector.

The medicine man fell to his knees with his head bowed. "I am no match for you, my wolf cannot defeat the Great Mother Bear. I concede. You win."

The people cheered as the teacher bestowed the title of medicine women on me. Grandpa, Grandma and Uncle were at the front of the crowd, cheering and beaming at me. Tears shone on Grandma's face. I was so excited I could hardly contain the feeling.

The joy and exhilaration was so strong it felt like it would burst out of my skin. I won, I was a medicine woman.

The End

Don't miss this excerpt from Maureen's next book.

Book 2

Shúhta Dene: Battle of Great Rock

Chapter One

Small Girl did not take being disqualified from the tests well. She raged around the village, screaming about how unfair it was and that she should have won the title of medicine woman. She turned to the dark, using everything at her disposal to seek revenge for what she saw filled her with constant rage in losing the title, Small Girl turns to the dark, seeking revenge for the embarrassment she felt tainted her family's name. She opened herself to the dark and welcomed it in.

* * *

Now that the title had passed to me Joe, the old medicine man stepped down and accepted me as the new medicine women. I wasn't sure what was involved and what I was supposed to do now. I went to Grandma and asked for her wisdom. We sat at the kitchen table while she explained.

"A healer's job is to see the future and seek visions of the past looking for answers to questions that plagued our community. I needed to gain more knowledge of the plants, and herbs, supply spiritual guidance for those who needed it. As a healer, you must look for spiritual guidance from the animals and especially your spirit guide. You must know and understand how to gather the ingredients and create the teas which help the sick heal. You must be able to control the clouds, although we cannot change the weather without dire consequences. Only Mother Nature has that power, and she keeps it to herself, but we can move the clouds if we need to. You must gain knowledge of the woods, the trails, and the mountains, learn to read where important information is hidden. Healers are the truth seekers and must be guided only by the light of positive energy. A healer must be in tune with the energy because it flows through all living things. A healer is often called upon rid the village or individuals of bad spirits that bring harm to others. Healers teach that there is good in all. Go'diah, if you truly believe in yourself and the gift you possess there is nothing you can't do. But with gifts such as these, be warned, if you lean toward the dark side and let the negative in, it will slowly eat away at your energy realm. It will consume you with madness in the search for power. Never let revenge or anger into your heart, no matter what the cost. It is never worth losing your soul or your mind over. We heal ourselves when we feel grief and sorrow. That is a challenge we as healers must always pay attention to. Never let negative thoughts into our minds, or it rots our core of goodness." Grandma patted my hand and took a drink of her tea.

My grandmother's words were so powerful and meaningful it opened my eyes to the negative side, the opposite of light is darkness. That was a line I never wanted to cross.

My grandpa came in from working on the smoke shed and we changed the subject to something less serious.

"It's a beautiful day, Moonshine. We hardly got any rain yet and the sun has melted most of the snow and dried up the puddles," Grandpa said smiling at her. "Do you want to have a cookout tonight?"

Grandma smiled back. "That sounds like a great idea." She turned to me. "Want to help me fix up stuff for cook out later?" she asked me.

I nodded yes and then went to my room. I needed to think about everything Grandma had told me. I threw myself on the bed, staring at the ceiling. My thoughts were spinning in my head. I was excited about my new position in the community, but at the same time, I was confused. I lay there, thinking to myself, this is crazy, how did all this happen?

One day everything was good. Normal. Then I tried to find help for Grandpa and I woke up all these things inside me when I went looking for the medicine. Things I never even knew were inside me. My solitary journey into the mountains set all this in motion. What about university now? I still wanted to go away after summer, start schooling to become a leader, educating myself to be able to help my village, but a medicine woman? What now? I couldn't just up and leave. The village would have no healer if I did that. Ugh! Everything was so messed up. I was after all only eighteen and that seemed too young to be taking on the role of medicine woman. I didn't know what to do. I sat up in bed and tried to connect with the teacher. I touched her mind but it seemed foggy and not as clear as I remembered. *I'll talk to you later*, she sent to me, *there is much to talk about, wait till I come.* Then, just like that the connection was gone. Ugh! I laid back down and thumped my pillow in frustration.

My door opened slowly. "I might be old, but I know when something is bothering you. May I come in?" Grandma asked.

I nodded yes. Grandma sat down on the bed beside me. "What is wrong?"

I looked at her sweet face and just couldn't tell her at the moment. I just kissed her head. "Grandma, I think I well take a short nap, I am tired."

She smiled, got up, and closed my curtain. "When do you want to get up?"

"In a few hours," I said looking at the time. It was only two in the afternoon.

Grandma closed my door and I fell into a deep sleep.

* * *

Small Girl

On the other side of the village, Small Girl was being yelled at by her father for failing in her quest to become medicine woman. Both of them are furious and a huge argument flares up between them. Small Girl couldn't stand being yelled at anymore and left the house to run into the forest.

She ran until her sides hurt and she couldn't' run anymore. She collapsed on the thick mat of leaves and needles on the ground and cried her heart out. Eventually, the hurt turned to anger. It's all Go'diah's fault, Small Girl seethed. Rage filled her, if Go'diah didn't suck up to the teacher, Small Girl would be medicine woman. The more she thought about it, the more the rage overwhelmed her. Her head came up with a start. Someone was called her name. Getting to her feet, Small Girl followed the voice. It led her far into the darkest part of the forest.

Finally, deep in the shadows, she saw an attractive young women, about Small Girl's age. The woman's long, beautiful hair flowed over her shoulders. Small Girl had never seen her before.

"I heard you crying. Why are you crying," the woman spoke gently as if she were speaking to a young child.

Not waiting for answer, the woman grabbed a tree branch and swung from it giggling. For some reason she didn't understand, Small Girl felt a strange connection with her.

"I failed a test and lost the title of medicine woman to a little *teacher's pet*," Small Girl snarled.

The strange girl laughed. "And now you want her to pay?"

Small girl looked up, somehow she knew her eyes had gone black as night. "Yes, oh yes. I want her to suffer for the embarrassment she caused me and my family."

The strange girl laughed. "Well, you came to the right place." She let go of the tree she was swinging on and led Small Girl to a hole in a ground big enough to hold both of them with room to spare.

"What is this place?" Small Girl asked.

The girl laughed but there was no humor in her voice. "This is your workplace, haven't you realized that yet?" She laughed again.

A wicked smile crossed Small Girl's face. The laugh that escaped her was grim. "I think the new medicine woman and I are about to become very close friends. I will learn how she did it even if it takes me a hundred years, and I will have my revenge."

* * *

The Friends (Go'diah)

The sun was out, and I was up early having a sip of coffee and enjoying the morning song of the birds. An elder approached me seeking my help.

"It's my granddaughter, she won't stop puking. I have tried everything I can think of. But nothing is working," the elder is upset.

"It will be okay," I tried to calm him down. "Wait here while I get my things, then I will come with you." I went into the back porch to mix up a batch of medicine that I thought would work. I had everything set up back there to mix my herbs. Grandpa had turned the entire back porch into a medicine work room for me. There was even a back door to for people to use. I looked up in surprise when Small Girl knocked on the front door. I was happy to see her. We had started getting closer in the past few months and she was the only that could understand what I was going through. Plus, it was nice having someone my own age to do stuff with.

"Come have some coffee, Small Girl," Grandma said.

Small Girl took a cup and while I was preparing the medicine, she told me her birthday was in a few weeks.

"Wouldn't it be nice to do something cool and hang out together," she suggested.

"Sounds like fun," I said.

Small Girl stood by my side, watching everything I did.

"What are you doing?"

"there's an elder waiting for me to come and help his sick granddaughter. I'm making a tea for her that should help."

She smiled and watched me really closely. I finished putting all the ingredients together. "Want to come with me?" I asked.

"Yes, of course," Small Girl said.

We left my house and went to the elder's house. The little girl wasn't doing very well. I gave her some sips of the medicine and gave her family instructions on how and when to give her more. They were grateful and tried to gift me with some Bannock.

"No, thank you. It is my job to help you and there is lots of food at my house. Thank you though for offering," I said.

When I turned to leave I noticed a glowering expression on Small Girl's face. It sent a chill through me and then I told myself I was being silly. I must have imagined it. But it kept bothering me as we walked back down the road toward my house.

"I saw that look on your face just before we left the elder's house, what was that about?"

She smiled but it didn't seem to reach her eyes. "It's nothing really, I was just thinking to myself that's all."

I watched her from the corner of my eye as we kept walking to my house. Something just wasn't setting right with me. What was bothering me about her? Nothing I could put my finger on, so I let it go. We spent the rests of the day together, making things, and helping people. Small Girl helped me and Grandma with the dried meat and the smoke shed.

"It's time to eat and call it a day," Grandma said. It was getting late in the day.

"I agree," I said.

"Good night," Small Girl said as she left.

Grandpa was outside and noticed her leave when he came inside the house he looked at me and frowned. "There's something not right about that kid," he said throwing his gloves down by the fire.

"She's just a kid and she likes hanging out here., Plus, its nice having that extra help," Grandma said. She smiled and kissed grandpa as she held him close.

I looked at them with a soft smile. They were just too cute together. It was time for bed, so we all went to our rooms.

Morning arrived with bird song outside my window. Grandma was talking in the kitchen and for some reason she sounded mad. I got up and headed to the kitchen. Grandma was bagging up all my herbs and plants and throwing them out.

"What are you doing to my medicine?" I rushed over to stop her.

She glared at me pointed to the porch. "Look!"

I stuck my head in the door and gasped. All my plants and herbs were burnt black. "What happened? It wasn't like this last night."

"Someone did this to you, and it's not good. Whoever did this doesn't want you helping anyone with your medicine. They have it out for you." Grandma kept bagging up the black ash that was all that was left of my herbs and plants.

I stared in disbelief. Who would do something like this? The more I thought about it the more upset I got. I was going to get to the bottom of this. I put my coat on and moved toward the door.

"Where are you off to?" Grandma stopped long enough to look at me.

"I need answers, and I'm going out to get some," I said.

I went over to the old medicine man's house and knocked hard on the door. His wife opened it.

"Go'diah, come in," she invited me.

Joe was in his rocker by the fire.

"Someone destroyed all my medicine plants and herbs last night. Who would do such a thing?" I asked him.

Joe looked confused, he threw back the blanket covering his legs and stood up. What are you talking about?"

I explained about the amount of damage done to my medicine supplies. "All that is left is a bunch of black ashes."

Joe gasped and rubbed his face with his hands. He waved a hand at his wife. "Lock the door," he ordered her.

She didn't hesitate but moved quickly to do as he asked.

"Come with me," he said. I followed him down the hallway to the last door. He opened it and went in. I trailed behind him. The room was full of all kinds of stuff, animal skulls, furs, hats, herbs, plants, a huge table for medicine making, candles, sage, and blankets, feathers. It was a lot to take in. Every piece of the wall was covered with something. Joe pulled out a box hidden under everything and looks at me.

"What you hear and see here in my home, you must never speak of to anyone," he said and was quite serious.

"I understand," I said.

He opened the box, inside was a head dress with some black ash on it. It looked like the ash at my house.

"I will tell you a story," he said. "Once I came across a healer in my travels to the other villages to help the sick. One day I got very sick myself. I was wearing this headdress when I was attacked by something not of this world. It was a warning to leave. I put the headdress in this box and took it to another wise healer. She was able to break the connection that the headdress had on me. The curse that was set on me. I keep this headdress as reminder that there those of us who carry the bloodline that practice anything other than goodness and light. I believe whoever did this to your medicines means to bring harm to you and your family," he finished the story.

"I have no clue who would do this to me," I said bewildered.

"Has anyone been with you lately that might have had access to your medicine supplies?" Joe regarded me with a worried frown.

I shook my head. "Just my family..." Then it dawned on me. "Small Girl knows the work I do and has been hanging out a lot lately since the teacher left," I whispered. I looked at the medicine man.

"Can you teach me how to find this person and send the threat back at them?" I asked.

Joe looked worried. "What you ask of me. It's not an easy thing to do. You must meditate on this." He explained what I needed to do. Wow, I had a lot of work to do I thought as he talked.

"You must go back into the mountains to pick more herbs and plants, then you must come back and came and see me," Joe said.

I went home and talked to my uncle. He agreed to travel with me to re supply myself again. We had just finished talking when a woman arrived.

"Go'diah, I need your help. You must come quickly," she gasped the words out.

I ran with her to her house. Inside, a boy close to my age was throwing up violently.

"Help him! He hasn't eaten anything strange or different. Just some bannock that was left on our doorstep two days ago. You know how people love to share in this village."

I pushed on his stomach, and he cried out. I knew I had to see what was happing with his insides. I took a deep breath and went into a trance. I found his energy; it was there but very weak. I watched the energy flowing through his body, I could see a thin black strand staining everything. I looked up at the woman.

"Get me lots of water. We need to bath him," I said, still holding the thread of energy.

The woman hurried to collect the supplies I needed. I had no medicines with me and there were none at home now either.

"You, " I said, pointing at the sick boy's brother, "go and get Joe the old medicine man." I scribbled on a bit of paper with a stub of a pencil. "Tell him this is what I need. He will know what to do." Thank God I had just been with him and knew he had the supplies that I needed. The brother raced out the door.

The mother came back with the supplies to bath her older son. We slipped the boy into the hip bath just as Joe came through the door. Joe didn't waste time on words, he knew what needed to be done. While the mother bathed her son, Joe and I mixed the herbs and boiled them until they were a black goo in the bottom of the pot over the fire.

Between us, we held the boy steady and poured the medicine down his throat. I had to hold his mouth shut to be sure it went all the way down to his stomach. He struggled and it took both Joe and I to hold him down. Then he calmed down and quit fighting. His eyes snapped open and he leaned over the side of the tub and puked up a bunch of nasty looking hair that writhed on the floor. It was disgusting to see it twitching and realize it came out the boy in the tub. Joe scooped it up and put it in a jar which he sealed tight.

"Nasty thing," he said, exchanging a serious look with me. "Good job thinking to ask me for help."

The boy was only the first of the villagers who got sick. Before the day was out people all over the community were getting sick. I was frustrated and angry that I had to rely on Joe for the medicines. Somehow I didn't think it was a coincidence that so many people were sick right at the same time my store of medicines was sabotaged. I got back home late that night. Uncle was waiting up for me.

"We need to go tomorrow. Joe can manage until we get back, but he will run out of medicine soon too, if we don't hurry back.

"We leave first thing in the morning. Now get some sleep, Go'diah. You look exhausted.

My books are based on my passion for the stories of myths & legends of witches and magic mixed with my wild and crazy imagination. The beautiful mountains that surrounded me as a child growing up in the north play a prominent role in my storytelling. I grew up respecting my culture and I am a proud Dene woman from the Northwest Territories.

I have always had an imagination, and I loved the stories elders told when I was growing up. When stories involved witches and magic I have always wanted to blend them with my people, the mountains, and my culture.